STRANGER AT GOLDEN HILL

Books by JOY DeWEESE WEHEN

———

STAIRWAY TO A SECRET

THE TOWER IN THE SKY

STRANGER AT GOLDEN HILL

Stranger at Golden Hill

by JOY DeWEESE WEHEN

WILDSIDE PRESS

For My Grandfather
TRUMAN ARMSTRONG DeWEESE
Author and Editor

Acknowledgment

To the late Judge Frederick C. Fisher of Ross, California, for his helpful advice on California Inheritance Law.

And to Mildred Brown Robbins, society editor of the San Francisco *Chronicle*, who generously shared her knowledge of the Debutante Cotillion ... My gratitude.

Contents

STRANGER AT GOLDEN HILL

CHAPTER ONE

Luncheon Invitation

THEY were just sitting down to breakfast when the door-bell rang.

"The mailman!" Melinda Marshall jumped up. " 'Scuse me, Mums."

Her mother looked after her with wonder. "How *can* Melinda always tell?"

"Miss Melinda got built-in radar for the postman, Mrs. Marshall," said Petunia, coming up from the kitchen. "Miss Honey Rose, here's your black coffee and orange juice," she added in a tone that left no doubt what she thought of people who had coffee and juice for breakfast instead of her famous sour-cream pancakes. Petunia had been with the Marshalls for so long that she was part of the family. She even made Mr. Marshall wear his rubbers when her little toe said that it was going to rain.

Meanwhile Melinda was racing down the stairs from the third-floor balcony where they breakfasted in the summer. Going on seventeen, she had wide amber eyes, an upturned nose and pointed chin, and hair the color of Petunia's caramel pralines.

August sunshine splashed through the high front windows as Melinda picked up the letters from under the slot. She

glanced through them, and sighed. Why did she tear downstairs for the mail when she wasn't expecting a special letter?
It was just that . . . well, someday there *might* be one for
her. From whom, she didn't know—and that was part of the
wonderfulness.

Meanwhile she would go on skidding down the banister
every morning when the postman rang. She laughed at herself
and went back up the stairs.

"They're all for you," she announced to her mother as she
prepared to bury her disappointment under seven pancakes.

"What can you expect, my pet," remarked Honey Rose,
"when your best friends are horses?"

Honey Rose Huntington was a cousin of Mrs. Marshall's
who put a lot of hard work into staying glamorous, slender
as a cattail, and twenty years old. She had come out from
Atlanta, Georgia, last Easter for a visit, and hadn't yet gotten
around to mentioning when she was going home.

Melinda grinned at her. "What's on the launching pad for
today? I feel like adventures."

"A hair appointment for me," replied Honey Rose, dropping saccharine in her coffee.

"Oh, not *again?*" groaned Melinda. "You can't waste a San
Francisco day like this in a beauty shop. Just look. . . ." She
swept her hand at the scene spread out before them.

Like many of the houses on Pacific Heights, the Marshall
home was only two stories high in front but four stories at the
back where the hill fell away. The porch where they were
having breakfast was built out from the third floor and shaded
by a towering eucalyptus tree. Beyond, like rows of birthday
boxes, white and pink and pale green houses were stacked up
and down the steep hills of San Francisco. A stiff-fingered

wind plucked the Bay into white caps; Marin County was tawny and violet in the sun; and beneath the scarlet ribbon of the Golden Gate Bridge, a fussy little freighter was setting off for Singapore.

"Glorious, darling," agreed Honey Rose, "but I'm still having my hair done."

Mrs. Marshall was opening her mail. "Bills, invitations, meetings." She sighed. "How glad I'll be to get away to the ranch tomorrow for a month. No committees, no entertaining. . . ."

"No entertaining?" exclaimed Honey Rose. "What about the barbecue for Melinda's birthday?"

"Oh, that's not entertaining, that's *fun*."

Melinda jumped up to give her pretty, platinum-haired mother a hug.

"Lindy, don't let me forget . . . Doña Ysabel wants us to bring up a new tire for the tractor."

Honey Rose stared. "Doña Ysabel . . . *tractor?*" she repeated, remembering Melinda's beautiful, fragile old Spanish godmother who lived at the Marshall ranch the year round.

Mrs. Marshall nodded. "Ysabel may not have left the ranch in fifty years, but she can still give Charles the latest developments in soil erosion and tell Petunia where to put the TV aerial to make the thing work . . . *and it does*," she added in awe. "I don't recognize this writing," she murmured, slitting the last envelope.

Inside was a note and another envelope. "Oh, that's Julia's writing. She's living in London now; this must be a letter of introduction." She read the two notes quickly. "Horrors!" she exclaimed. "She wants us to meet 'a delightful young friend' who is visiting America. And the friend asks if we could come to lunch at the Canterbury on the tenth . . . that's today! And I have that committee meeting this morning and there's the party tonight. We've invited too many girls already. And tomorrow the ranch. Whatever shall I do?"

"What's her name, Mums?"

Mrs. Marshall studied the letter, tilting it from side to side. "Well, you know Julia's writing. A string of smudges and a tadpole's tail. I *think* it's Ruby Sutherland. See what you can make of it."

She handed the sheets across the table. Melinda squinted at them, wondering how her mother had deciphered that much. To her, it looked as though the visitor went by the rather original name of *Rummmmmmmm Suuunnnnnd*.

She turned to the letter, written in crisp italic handwriting:

> Dear Mrs. Marshall,
> I hope you will forgive this short notice, but I am not sure how long I shall be in the Bay Area. Could you and your daughter—and your husband if he is free—join me for luncheon on the tenth of August, about one o'clock? I am staying at the Hotel Canterbury in Sutter Street.
> Hoping to have the pleasure of meeting you then,
> Yours,
> R. SUTHERLAND

Melinda handed back the letters. "I wish my writing looked like that," she said.

"So do I," agreed her mother with feeling. "I have an idea," she exclaimed: "You and Honey Rose go instead. Then, if you like Ruby Sutherland, we could invite her up to the ranch."

"Well-l-l . . ." It wasn't exactly the sort of adventure Melinda had had in mind, but it was something. "All right with me. Can you change your hair appointment, Honey Rose?"

The Southern girl shook her head with a lazy smile. "Sorry, my pet, Honey Rose Huntington never changed any appointment . . . to meet a *girl!*"

And so it was that, a couple of hours later, Melinda set out by herself, in a blue linen dress with a gay raincoat on her arm, as a summer fog often settles over San Francisco in the late afternoon.

On each side as she walked to the bus were tall houses standing shoulder to shoulder, with tiny butter-pat gardens in front. There wasn't an inch to spare in Pacific Heights now, where less than a hundred years ago patches of blue lupine quilted the sand dunes against the wind, and picnickers had gathered wild strawberries on the salt-swept headlands called Sea Cliff.

Melinda got out of the bus at Sutter and then crossed Polk Street—Polk was the president under whom California became part of the Union—to reach the Canterbury. She suddenly found herself looking forward to this luncheon. She had never known any English girls. Perhaps Ruby would love horses, too.

She smiled a thank you at the doorman as he held the door for her, and then looked around the lobby. But there were only two elderly ladies in a corner and a man buying a paper at the desk. Glancing at her watch, she sat down on the sofa by the window. She was five minutes early.

Absently she let her eyes wander around the room. At the desk, the man finished paying for his paper and turned around. Melinda watched him; she liked studying people. He was tall, with wavy hair, a no-nonsense jaw, and deep blue eyes. Honey Rose would probably have labeled him dreamy, she thought. She glanced at his eyes again, blue as bachelor buttons . . . and then realized for the first time that he was also looking at her.

Quickly she lowered her eyes, her cheeks turning pink. She hadn't meant to stare like that.

And then, to her dismay, he started to walk toward her.

What had she brought on herself? She glanced in panic around the lobby. Where, oh, where, was Ruby Sutherland?

The man was standing in front of her. Melinda had just screwed up her courage to survey him in cool and distant surprise when from somewhere out of the clouds far above her head an English accent exclaimed: "You're Melinda Marshall, aren't you? I'd know you anywhere from your aunt's picture of you. I'm so glad that you were able to make it."

With a quick, boyish smile he held out his hand. "I'm Robin Sutherland."

CHAPTER TWO

Peril in a Narrow Street

MELINDA was so stunned that it was a whole second before she could take his outstretched hand.

Then. "But—but you're a *man!*" she blurted out. Which was, of course, the last thing in the world she meant to say.

Robin Sutherland stared at her. "Well, yes, I'm afraid so." Then his blue eyes began to twinkle. "Don't you like men, Miss Marshall? I'm awfully sorry. Perhaps I could persuade you to change your mind."

Melinda turned a shade pinker and she drew a deep breath. She *must* pull herself together before he gave her up as feeble-minded. But the one sentence that kept buzzing around in her head was no help—the delicious, uncousinly thought: *Just wait until Honey Rose hears what she missed!*

She gave herself a swift shake and put on her most poised voice. "Aunt Julia's writing is such a squiggle, you see, that we read your name as *Ruby*. And you didn't help by only signing your name *R. Sutherland.*"

"So that's it!" The young Englishman threw back his head, laughing. "No wonder you looked startled."

Melinda laughed with him, her embarrassment melting under his naturalness. "Mums was so sorry that she couldn't come, too, but she had a committee meeting. And Hon ..."

She stopped. Why tell him about Honey Rose? He'd meet her soon enough. Meanwhile, well, Robin Sutherland was *her* property for one afternoon. "So she asked me to give you her regrets."

"The regret is mine," replied Robin gallantly. But he didn't look as though he were pining away. "Now, item number one: lunch." He helped her up from the sofa. "Where would you like to go? You know San Francisco better than I do."

As they went out of the door it suddenly seemed to Melinda that the sunshine was much more golden and sparkling than when she went in. She wondered how ten minutes could make such a difference.

"What about birds' nests and sharks' fins?" she asked him.

"Er . . . I beg your pardon?"

"Birds' nests and sharks' fins," she repeated mischievously.

"I *thought* that was what you said," murmured Robin, shaking his head. "I know I'm not very bright, my Oxford tutors kindly made that clear many times, but . . ."

Melinda's laughter bubbled up. "They're Chinese dishes. I was really asking if you'd like to have luncheon in China-town?"

"I'd love it," answered Robin eagerly. "That's a wizard idea. I've been longing to see Chinatown. Is it far? Shall we take my car?"

Melinda looked up at him in surprise. "Oh, no, we can walk. But have you a car?"

"Well, you might call it that if you were being extra polite. I only know that I drove across the continent in something with four wheels and forty squeaks."

"What kind is it?"

"I call it an MG, but my friends call it a Menace. Its name is Lightnin' Bug."

"Lightnin' Bug?" Melinda's nose crinkled in delight. "Why?"

"There's a slight difference of opinion over that, I'm afraid," replied Robin solemnly. "I bestowed the name to celebrate the car's remarkable speed and brilliance, also in honor of its complexion, which is bright yellow. Unfortunately, it is thought by some subversive characters to refer to the head-lights which do ... er ... flicker at times!"

Melinda liked listening to him talk. His accent was crisply English, not the affected kind that Daddy called "playing the crumpet." "I'd love to see it."

"You shall," promised Robin. "I only hope you love it *when* you've seen it."

In a few minutes they turned down Grant Avenue, named for the president who had once been just a homesick young army officer stationed in Northern California. Now it's the main street of the largest Chinese colony in the world outside of the Orient. Melinda and Robin found themselves in a different world, with carved balconies and tilt-tiled roofs, narrow, mysterious alleys, and dragon-twined street lamps. Shopwindows displayed brocades, slit-skirted Chinese dresses, and the precious emerald-flecked jade called Pine Needles on Snow. Enticing smells of coconut, lichee nuts, and ginger advertised a candy shop. In a butcher's window hung tightly trussed ducks varnished to the glossy brownness of mahogany. Overhead floated the wailing notes of a Chinese song, monoto-nous yet strangely urgent. An old Chinese woman trudged past them in a Pekin-blue dress, her hair scraped into a bun, a

fortune in gold bracelets on her wrist. Clinging to her hand was a little Chinese boy in complete cowboy outfit waving a paper dragon on a stick.

"East meets Wild West!" laughed Robin. "I never . . ." He broke off to stop short in front of a shopwindow. "Melinda," he demanded in horror, "what are those?"

Melinda peered through the dusty glass. "Hmmm, those are

dried octopuses, I mean octopi. I never can decide which sounds more appetizing: *pussies* or *pie*. Then that next saucer—probably a particular potent spider. And of course if it's a really good Chinese drugstore, there'll be tigers' whiskers and powdered rhinoceros horn, and . . ."

"Stop!" implored Robin. "Don't tell me any more until after luncheon."

Melinda led him away from the window, saying wickedly: "After the sort of luncheon I'm going to order for you you'll need a prescription of ground beetles and a nice dried lizard or two. We're nearly there."

They turned down a steep, narrow side street, deserted except for a few cars and a big truck parked at the top of the hill. The buildings were close together here, shuttered and secretive after the bright shops and vivid banners of Grant Avenue. A dirty, dignified gray cat sat on a window sill and looked at them with eyes the color of aquamarines.

"It's less crowded the minute you leave Grant Avenue," said Melinda. "That's why we like this little restaurant off the tourist track. The Chinese eat here. The food is the real thing and. . . . Why, what's that?"

She stopped as a sudden thundering rumble shook the pavement behind them.

The only two people in the narrow street, they turned quickly, just in time to see the big truck above them set off down the hill.

Melinda looked at it . . .

And a cold hand closed around her heart. *There was no driver behind the wheel!* The brakes had lost their hold on the slippery hill. The huge vehicle had broken loose.

Melinda clutched Robin's arm in terror as the rumble mounted to a scream of tires. Faster and faster the runaway truck hurtled down the steep incline toward them.

With a cry, the dirty gray cat fled from its window sill.

CHAPTER THREE

Whisper in Chinatown

J UMP!" shouted Robin. He snatched Melinda into a
   doorway.

The truck caught the fender of a parked car. With a shatter
of glass, the car crumpled like cellophane. Speed checked for
an instant, the truck swerved, and . . .

"Robin, stop!" screamed Melinda.

But with a running jump Robin had leaped onto the truck's
step. Wrenching the door open, he dived across to the driver's
seat. While the truck careened on down the hill, he fought to
pull the gears into low. Melinda watched, her heart in her
throat.

The gears finally gripped with a screech, and for the first
time Robin dared to hope that he could bring the truck to a
safe stop at the next level crossing.

And then he saw the bus.

It was a school bus filled with children. The driver was halfway across the intersection when he saw the truck plunging
toward him. In panic he jammed on his brakes . . . and the bus
stopped squarely in Robin's path.

Robin lunged for the emergency brake. Skidding tires
clawed the pavement in black zigzags, but the hill was too
steep.

Hands frozen on the steering wheel, the bus driver braced for the crash.

There was none.

At the corner of the street stood a warehouse with a high brick wall. Deliberately Robin swung the steering wheel around and crashed the truck, and himself, into it.

Melinda moved through the next few hours in a curious unreality—like looking at pictures in someone else's scrapbook.

First the police arrived, followed by the trembling owner of the truck (who swore that he had left the brake on and the wheels cramped into the curb), and the once-deserted street filled with swarms of Chinese, sight-seers, photographers, and reporters. A moment later an ambulance sirened through the crowd. Over his energetic protests Robin was whisked to Emergency Hospital for a checkup. "What nonsense, I only scraped my knee a bit."

Melinda went with him, then sat numbly in the hospital waiting room, drinking the coffee a nurse brought her, trying to realize that the handsome young Englishman she had known for less than a morning might now be the hero of San Francisco.

But after an examination confirmed only the scraped knee —"a miracle," said one of the doctors—Robin and Melinda were able at last to slip out of a side door where a police car was waiting to take them to the little Chinese restaurant for which they were originally headed. *So long ago*, thought Melinda, *was it really only two hours?*

At the cafe, they made their way to a booth at the back, hoping that no one had spotted them. "I've had enough reporters to last me for the rest of my life," muttered Robin.

Except for a few framed scrolls of black characters on red silk the tiny restaurant was as clean and bare as the inside of a camphorwood box. From their table they caught a glimpse of the kitchen. Crowded with wicker baskets of bean sprouts, ripply skirted mushrooms, Chinese cabbage, bowls of chopped pork, and perky pink shrimps, it was presided over by a genial cook who displayed his fortune in gold teeth every time he smiled.

As they sat down, Melinda impulsively reached across the table and laid her hand on Robin's arm. "I promise not to bring it up again, Robin, but I've got to say it once. You were so wonderful. You saved my life and ... and all those children. You might have been killed. Oh, Robin"—her voice caught—"there are no words ... big enough."

"N-n-nonsense, Melinda." His color deepened. "I only d-d-did what anybody else would have done in my place. Anyway, it's all over; don't think about it. Everything's t-t-tickety-boo now!"

She withdrew her hand, noticing that Robin stammered shyly when he was embarrassed. It was oddly attractive. "Tickety-boo?" she repeated.

"English slang for okay!" He grinned. Then, looking up to find the Chinese waiter standing by their table, he went on very slowly and distinctly, "We likee soup chop-chop. Can do?"

Without a flicker of expression the waiter took out his pencil. "What sort of soup would you care for, sir? I can give you melon-ball, sharks' fin, egg flower, and mushroom with water chestnut. I can particularly recommend the melon-ball today."

Melinda stifled giggles at Robin's astonishment. "Sorry," he gulped. "I'm afraid that sounded rather rude, but I didn't mean it that way. Where did you learn to speak such good English?"

"I was born here, sir, and so were my parents. I'm working my way through the university."

Robin swallowed. "Er . . . you *do* speak Chinese?" he asked cautiously.

For the first time the young waiter's face broke into a quick grin. "Pidgin Chinese, sir!"

They settled for the melon-ball soup, duck with almonds, fried rice, butterfly shrimps, and spareribs in a sweet-sour sauce.

"And chopsticks, please," added Melinda.

"Oh, I say, Melinda," pleaded Robin, "have mercy on a poor starving foreigner."

"They're easy," Melinda assured him, "and Chinese food just doesn't taste the same with a knife and fork."

"How right you are," agreed Robin a minute later after three valiant attempts to pick up a slithery sparerib with the bamboo sticks, "this way you never taste it at all."

"Just pretend they're a fountain pen," Melinda showed him. "Keep the lower one steady and the upper one movable for grasping things. It's really easy."

"If you say that once more, Miss Marshall," threatened Robin, "I'll make you eat haggis with a dirk when you come to Britain!"

But after a few minutes' practice he managed a couple of bites. He laid down his chopsticks. "Writer's cramp," he explained, and looked across at Melinda. "You know, your aunt didn't tell me an awful lot about you, except that you were sixteen and had hair the color of sunshine. Shouldn't we fill in the gaps?"

"I'll really be seventeen next week," Melinda corrected him hastily. Somehow it was most important that Robin should know she was almost seventeen. "Then, let's see, I was born here in San Francisco, and . . ."

"Oh, then you're a native Californian?"

Melinda took a demure sip of tea. "I'm not a Suisún Indian, if that's what you mean. But my forebears came with Anza almost two hundred years ago."

"Who was Anza?"

Melinda's eyes opened in amazement. Surely *everybody* knew about Juan Bautista de Anza, "the greatest colonial administrator in history," as her schoolbooks called him? "Anza was the man who discovered a land route from Mexico to California," she told him. "So the Spanish government—Mexico belonged to Spain then—gave him the job of colonizing the new country. He picked two hundred and forty people, and in 1776 they arrived here after the long trek from Sonora in Mexico."

"You mean—" Robin picked up his chopsticks again—"that California started here in the West at just the same time that the United States was being born on the eastern seaboard? I never realized that. But you know, Melinda," he went on wickedly, gazing at her honey-colored hair, "you don't look like a Mexican!"

"Well, there have been a few events since." She laughed. "Such as the captain of an English sailing vessel falling in love with one of my umpty-great grandmothers and settling down here to take over the family rancho." As the waiter brought almond cakes and fortune cookies for dessert, Melinda added,

"Most of the great California families began when ships' officers from England and Boston married daughters of Spanish-Mexican landowners out here and settled down in the New World."

"Why did so many ships come here?" asked Robin, "apart from the señoritas?"

"*Fur,*" replied Melinda. "The sea-otter trade with China. That was a huge business; almost every nation tried to horn in on it. Even the Russians. They bought a tract of land up along the Mendocino coast and started a settlement."

Robin stared at her. "You mean that the Russian flag once flew over California soil?"

"For twenty years. Then the Russians abandoned their Fort Ross. But the United States got so worried over that particular colony that President Monroe drew up his famous Monroe Doctrine, warning Europe to keep hands off of the Americas. . . . Oh, Robin, what does it say? Let me see."

Robin was opening his fortune cookie. Suddenly he burst out laughing. "It says BEWARE, IT IS LATER THAN YOU THINK." He glanced at his watch. "Probably the polite Chinese way of letting us know that it's nearly four o'clock!"

"Goodness, is it?" exclaimed Melinda. "I never dreamed . . ."

"Neither did I. Delightful luncheon . . . and good luck with your degree," he added to the waiter as they left the restaurant.

Without realizing it they found themselves returning up the street of the runaway truck. But all traces of the accident had been cleared away. There remained only the hole in the warehouse wall where Robin had crashed the huge vehicle. However, there were still a lot of people standing around at the top of the narrow street, talking and pointing.

"Bit of a squash through here," commented Robin, "perhaps we'd better go single file."

He fell back a step or two.

And then somehow they became separated. One minute Robin was there, close to her shoulder. The next minute Melinda looked around and couldn't see him.

Instead, padding so close behind her that she jumped, was a Chinese. He was looking at her intently, not fleetingly, like someone in a crowd. It was only a sliver of time that his face was so close to hers, but it was like the snap of a shutter. For the rest of her life every detail was photographed on Melinda's memory, down to the drooping left eyelid.

A little frightened, she didn't know why . . . she pulled her gaze away and with an effort stood on tiptoe to search for Robin.

The Englishman was only a few feet away, after all, wedging his way through the throng. Ridiculously relieved, she waved.

But before Robin could rejoin her, a soft whisper brushed her ear.

"There is a Chinese proverb, Miss Marshall: *To trust a stranger is to walk a dark road without a lantern.*"

Melinda whirled. But the man with the drooping eyelid had disappeared into the crowd.

CHAPTER FOUR

Introductions

WHAT'S the matter?" asked Robin. "You look as though you'd seen a ghost." Taking her arm, he guided her into Grant Avenue.

There was no sign anywhere of the Chinese with the drooping eyelid.

"I . . . I . . ." Melinda hesitated. She couldn't tell Robin about that chilling whisper. Not yet. Not until she found out what it meant. How had an unknown Chinese known her name? What was he talking about? Above all, who was the "stranger"?

"Yes?" prompted Robin.

Melinda pulled herself together. "It—it was hard to talk in that crowd." She looked up at him: arrow tall, straight blue eyes, a hero in a crisis. And yet—*how little she knew him.* Barely three hours. A friend of a scatterbrained aunt eight thousand miles away. How did she know who he really was? What he was doing here in San Francisco? Could *he* be the "stranger"?

She forced her voice to be light. "Anyway, it's your turn now, Robin. You haven't told me anything about yourself or . . . or why you came to California."

"That's easy," replied Robin. "Born in the North of England. Educated at Winchester, and Magdalen College, Oxford. Service in the Guards. At present seeing the world with the flimsy excuse of writing an article or two. Not much to tell, I'm afraid." He grinned. "What about you? Are you in college?"

He said it naturally, but Melinda noticed that he had turned the conversation away from himself again.

She shook her head. "I've just graduated from high school. I'm making my debut at Christmas, but next year I hope to go to Stanford."

"How do you make a debut in this country? There's no queen to curtsy to."

"No, but there's presentation at the Cotillion. And Mums is giving an old-fashioned tea for me. Will you still be here in December?"

"I should very much like to be," replied Robin eagerly. "It all depends..." But he didn't explain exactly what it depended upon.

They had just reached the corner of California Street when suddenly from their left came a frolicking set of notes on a gong: *pom tiddly-um, pom POM.*

Robin glanced around in surprise. He saw only a sedate red-brick church and beyond that an even more sedate insurance company. Neither of them, in Robin's view, a *tiddly-um POM* sort of place.

He had just begun, "Melinda, whatever's that..." when he spotted it: a gay little streetcar puffing up the hill. As the gripman tugged on his rope in a final flourish, pulling down a whole shower burst of *pom-POMS* from the gong above him, the trolley rocked to a stop in the middle of the intersection.

"That's one of our San Francisco cable cars," announced Melinda proudly.

Robin started to say, "It looks more like a cartoon by Emett to me," and then decided that that might not be the most polite-visitor thing to say, so he changed it to, "Really? I haven't ridden one yet."

"Oh, Robin, you *must!* This one's going our way. Let's catch it."

Dashing across the street, they jumped up the steep step to the outside seats ranged on either side of the gripman.

"Hold on tight going up the hill," Melinda warned Robin.

As the next moment he found himself sliding down the slippery wooden seat toward her, Robin obediently grabbed the pole in front of him. "What is this, Mount Everest?"

"No, it's Nob Hill," called back Melinda against the buzzing of the cable in its slot between the tracks under them. "This was where all the millionaires had their mansions before the fire ... the 'Nobs.' "

"What are Nobs?" asked Robin.

"Oh, people who made money in the continental railway like Leland Stanford and Mark Hopkins. Or they struck it rich in the Comstock Bonanza in the sixties, when silver was found in Nevada. Mr. Flood, for instance, owned half of a saloon here in San Francisco where the prospectors came when they were in town. He listened to their talk and picked up tips on what mining stock to buy, and six years later he and his partner were worth three hundred million dollars and building mansions on Nob Hill with gold water faucets!"

"I say, Melinda," Robin interrupted her, "just a minor detail—but where are we going now?"

Melinda looked at him in dismay. "I forgot! You're staying

at the Canterbury. I go on to the end of the line. But you'd better get off at the next stop and walk down the hill."

"Why don't you come with me, and I'll get the car and drive you home?"

"Oh, thank you, but . . ." She paused. A certain bright idea was taking shape in her mind. Mums had given too many girls already as her reason for not inviting "Ruby" Sutherland to the party tonight. But if she knew that it was really *Robin* Sutherland and a very attractive Robin Sutherland at that, just perhaps she might change her mind. Melinda stole a sideways glance at him. The wind was ruffling his wavy hair, and his eyes were as clear and blue as a Devon sky. Pushing dark whispers in Chinatown to the back of her mind, she took the plunge. "Mums is giving a small party this afternoon, it's from six to eight. Would you like to come?" she asked all in one breath.

Robin turned quickly. "Like it? I'd love it." The warmth in his voice showed that he really meant it. "But are you quite sure that your f-f-family . . . ?"

"Quite sure," replied Melinda, crossing her fingers in the pocket of her coat. "Come about six."

"Righto. Thanks awfully for asking me."

As the cable car swayed to a stop, Robin swung down off the high step.

"Thank *you* for a lovely luncheon," Melinda called after him. She started to add, "And thank you for saving my life," but that sounded flippant and not at all the way she meant it, so she just waved instead.

Punctually that evening, as the clock in the hall was clearing its throat with a whir to strike six, there was an earsplitting roar and Lightnin' Bug pulled up in front of the Marshall house.

Melinda was in her mother's room, having her blue silk print zipped up the back. She had told Mums about the afternoon—all but that whisper—and although Mrs. Marshall had turned rather white and sat down quickly on the edge of the bed when Melinda came to the runaway truck (she couldn't minimize it, her parents would see the papers), she had only said "Oh, Baby!" and then drawn a deep breath. "I'm so glad you invited him tonight. *Ruby* Sutherland. Just wait until I write to Julia!"

Honey Rose had not come home yet. Melinda was enjoying the thought of her cousin's face when she came in and found Robin there.

Melinda had told her mother all about Robin, but she had forgotten to mention Lightnin' Bug. So when what sounded like a jet fighter zoomed up the street, Mrs. Marshall jumped from her chair. "Whatever was that?"

Melinda peeked over her shoulder. In front of the house was parked a not-too-young MG with one rakish fender. It wasn't "bright" yellow as Robin had called it; it was a blinding, bouncing yellow.

Even Melinda blinked. "I ... I guess that's Lightnin' Bug," she faltered.

Mrs. Marshall's eyebrows rose. "All these modern vitamins and things," she murmured. "When I last saw a lightning bug twenty years ago I'm sure it wasn't that big."

Laughing, Melinda stepped back from the window as Robin got out of the car. He had changed to a dark suit and one of those sober British ties that look so restrained next to an exuberant American design, and yet tell a proud and sometimes exciting story of school or university or regiment.

"Well, darling," exclaimed Mrs. Marshall after one look, "if that's whom you've been talking about, English understatement must be catching. You told me that he was *sort of good-looking.*" She gave her daughter's cheek a pat as they went downstairs together. "*I* think he's devastating!"

Melinda skipped a step.

As Petunia went to answer the bell, Melinda found her heart beating a little faster. But she had no time for shyness, for all at once Robin was coming toward them, his warm smile lighting up the hall.

"Good evening, Melinda." He bowed over her hand and Melinda found herself thinking of that rare Old-World word "chivalrous."

She turned. "Mums, may I present Robin Sutherland? My mother, Mrs. Marshall."

Robin was just saying, "It's very good of you to let me come like this," and Mrs. Marshall was answering, "My dear Mr. Sutherland, any Ruby who turned into a Robin would be more than welcome in this house of girls!" when there was the sound of a key in the front door.

Melinda turned quickly, expecting her father.

But it was Honey Rose.

She looked lovely, as always, tall and willow slender against the open door behind her. She had a dress box in one hand. With the other she took off her dark glasses.

Melinda stole a glance at Robin. He was looking at Honey Rose, of course. But he didn't have that goggle-eyed expression Melinda was used to seeing on her college friends' faces when they were first exposed to Honey Rose. He seemed to be reserving judgment, waiting for her to say something.

Which she did.

Only, unfortunately, not in her usual creamy drawl. Shutting the door behind her sharply, she demanded, "What's that rattletrap sardine can doing in front of this house? Whose is it?"

CHAPTER FIVE

The Baron de Palafox

I ... I beg your pardon?" murmured Robin.
Honey Rose jumped. "Wh-what?"

Mrs. Marshall hurried to her rescue. "Honey Rose, this is Robin Sutherland. Our cousin, Honey Rose Huntington."

Honey Rose's eyes opened wide. "*Robin* Sutherland?" But she recovered swiftly. "I was only joking, truly, Mr. Sutherland," she said, her voice all candied violets again. "I just *love* British sports cars, really."

A smile twitched Robin's upper lip. "My MG has been called far worse names than a rattletrap sardine can. Please don't apologize."

"I'm *so* happy to meet you ... " But before Honey Rose could finish, the doorbell rang again with the first of the party guests. "Oh, dear, am I that late? Be with you in a minute." She hurried up the stairs.

Melinda couldn't resist the temptation of going with her. As soon as they were out of earshot, she said sweetly: "Your hair looks lovely, Honey Rose. Aren't you glad you had it done instead of coming to lunch with us?"

Honey Rose glared at her. But it wasn't a very fierce glare, and they both burst out laughing. Honey Rose put her arm around Melinda's shoulders. "I guess it just isn't my day, pet.

And he's so attractive, too. *Ruby* Sutherland! My, that was cruel!"

Several people had arrived when Melinda returned to the living room. She caught sight of Robin surrounded by guests and heard the exclamation: "How brave of you!" Her heart sank—of course everybody had seen the evening papers. Poor Robin!

In a minute he broke away and joined her. "I thought you were never coming! I need you."

"What for?" She felt a little tingle at his words.

"For five minutes of *not* talking about that runaway lorry."

"Would you like to see the famous view from our hanging porch instead?"

At his eager nod she led the way up to the wide balcony off the third floor. In the afternoon light the long, curved leaves of the eucalyptus strummed the breeze like fingers on a harp.

Petunia came out after them, carrying a tray of glasses. Robin chose ginger ale and Melinda glanced up in surprise. "In the books I've read Englishmen always take scotch and soda."

Robin grinned. "Then it's time you read some ginger-ale books!" He clicked his glass against her Coke. "Here's to the Golden West!" he said, looking at her hair, bright as a five-dollar gold piece in the sun.

Before Melinda could reply, an older man joined them on the porch. Although he moved with difficulty on wooden crutches, he looked like a Gay Nineties dandy. He had a gray mustache and pointed goatee; his waistcoat was jonquil yellow; there was a rose in his buttonhole.

"Oh, *ma chère amie*, they tell me you are up here. I am *enchanté* to see you."

"Baron," exclaimed Melinda, "I'm so glad you got back in time for the party."

"Ze university, they ask me to give some lectures in California history at the summer school, so 'ere I am." He glanced inquiringly at Robin.

Quickly Melinda introduced the two men. The baron seemed delighted to meet what he called "our 'ero," although Robin winced. Robin, in turn, learned that the Baron Henri de Palafox was a Frenchman whose specialty was California history and that he had made his home in San Francisco for the past seven years.

"Most hospitable city in the world," he informed Robin. "On my first visit I do not know one single . . . how you say it . . . spirit."

"Soul," suggested Melinda.

"But within a week, *voilà*, more invitations that I can accept!" He paused to dip a potato chip into the bowl of *guacamole*, a Mexican spread made of whipped and seasoned avocado.

"They're certainly hospitable here, sir, I can vouch for that," Robin agreed, smiling across at Melinda.

"*Naturellement*, it is a tradition," explained the older man. "In the days of the dons, a traveler was welcome to stay at any rancho or hacienda for a day—or a year."

"What was the difference between a rancho and a hacienda, sir?" asked Robin. "I've often wondered."

"Haciendas raised crops; ranchos raised cattle. The estates were huge, thousands of acres."

Melinda smiled to herself. When the baron started one of his lectures on California history, any attempt at changing the subject was like trying to deflect the Mississippi with a tea-spoon.

"The golden era of California," he went on, and his voice dropped to a tone of such convincing nostalgia that if Melinda had not known that the "days of the dons" were from the 1830's to 1849, she would have thought that the baron was looking back upon a treasured childhood memory. "Vast sun-drenched estates, prosperity, leisure, contentment. No poverty, no slums, no worry. . . ."

"And no schools, no post office, no libraries, no newspapers, no shops, and no plumbing either!" Melinda couldn't resist adding.

The baron went on without even noticing her. "Cattle was king. Hides were called 'California banknotes' because all trade was barter. Although most of the *estancias* made every-thing they needed, from candles to carriages. Forgive me," he broke off apologetically, "I am boring you."

"Oh, no, you're not, sir," replied Robin. In spite of the baron's schoolroom manner Robin was fascinated by these glimpses of the early West. The land they recalled, timeless, sunswept, unlimited, was so different from his own small island that wore her crowded past like a coat of many colors. Here history was a ranchero's sweep of scarlet cape across the empty hills. . . .

"But I'm afraid we're taking too much of your time," put in Melinda. "Mums will be wondering if we've kidnaped you!"

"*Oui, oui,* you are right. We must return to the so-charming party."

As they went back into the house, Robin murmured in Melinda's ear, "I say, how does he manage the stairs?"

"It's wonderful what he can do," whispered back Melinda, "even though he's been lame all his life."

The living room was crowded when they returned. But Melinda spotted her father who had just come home, and she took Robin up to introduce him. Mr. Marshall was a tall man with a dry smile and an air of patient good humor. He greeted Robin with a warm handshake. "Good to have you with us. . . ." Then he was interrupted by new arrivals.

A moment later Robin felt a light touch on his arm. "Aren't you even going to *speak* to me?" pleaded Honey Rose.

Robin smiled and looked down at her. Looking at Honey Rose was never hard. With her misty-black hair and pale, perfect skin, she was a striking girl. Robin would have called her beautiful except for her eyes. Dark and expressive as they were, they lacked serenity. They had a flitting restlessness that contrasted with her languid movements and lazy voice. He thought of Melinda's steady gaze.

"What part of the South are you from, Honey Rose?" he asked her.

Five minutes later a bewildered Robin realized that he had chosen the right subject. He was dizzy from Honey Rose's account of who the Huntingtons were and who her great-uncle was on her mother's side, and whom her grandfather's sister had married, not to mention what Civil War battles they had all fought in.

Melinda, who was busy helping her mother and Petunia, glanced wistfully across the room at them. Honey Rose was obviously giving Robin what Daddy called "the moonlight and magnolia works," and Robin didn't look as though he exactly *minded*.

"Why Melinda Marshall, you should be ashamed of your-self," she said firmly.

At half-past eight the party began to thin out. Regretfully Robin told Mrs. Marshall and Melinda that he must go.

Mrs. Marshall tucked her daughter's hand through her arm. "Darling, I've asked Robin if he couldn't come up to the ranch over your birthday. He mustn't leave the Bay Area without seeing the Valley of the Moon and an authentic California house." She turned to Robin. "El Rancho de la Colina de Oro was originally a Spanish rancho, and though it's been modern-ized, we haven't let it show!"

A flush of gratitude had spread under Robin's tan. "I c-c-can't think of anything I'd l-l-love to do more, Mrs. Marshall."

"Then come up tomorrow around noon and..." She paused, lifting her hand to her forehead in a gesture that was known in the Marshall household as shshsh-everybody-Mums-is-thinking. "Melinda tells me that you have a car."

"She exaggerated, ma'am," returned Robin, "but it was very flattering."

"We always have so much stuff to take up to the ranch. Do you think you could manage a box and some riding boots?"

"I'd be delighted to help. By the way, how do I get to the Valley of the Moon? By rocket?"

"Oh, dear." Mrs. Marshall knitted her pretty brows. "Of course you don't know where it is. And the house *is* hard to find."

"May I suggest something, Mrs. Marshall?" asked Robin,

unaccountably coloring again. "Why don't I take a passenger as well? It would give you more space, and she could direct me. I m-m-mean, whoever it is."

Mrs. Marshall looked at him, and a smile tilted her mouth. "What a good idea. I'll tell Honey Rose."

Robin looked surprised. "Wouldn't Melinda know the way better?" he said quickly.

It was Mrs. Marshall's turn to look surprised. She also looked pleased. "All right with you, Lindy?"

"Why, yes, I think it's a good idea." Melinda's voice was very matter-of-fact, but she was amazed to find that she was still on the ground and not floating up among the prisms of the chandelier.

"Then could you . . . Oh, Baron, must you go?" Mrs. Marshall broke off as the Frenchman joined the little group in the hall.

Balancing on his crutches, he bent over her hand. "Delightful party, my dear Helen, as always."

"I hope we'll see you again, Henri. We're going up to the ranch for a month. Where are you off to?"

"Tomorrow—Santa Rosa for a lecture."

"Why don't you drive over the following day? We're having a birthday barbecue for Melinda."

The baron bowed. "*Enchanté*. Colina de Oro is a corner of paradise." He turned to Robin. "And what do you do with yourself, monsieur, during your visit? You see San Francisco?"

"A little later, sir. The Marshalls have most kindly invited me to visit them at the ranch, too."

"Wonderful, wonderful." The baron beamed.

"Then I've been asked to write some articles on California;

and I mean to do some research on the period around 1840 in California history."

At the word "history," the older man was all attention. "Excellent, excellent." (Robin wondered if the baron's adjectives, like policemen, always traveled in pairs.) "If there is anything I can do ... introductions, a card to private libraries. . . ."

"Thanks awfully, sir, but I'm afraid I won't have time to go into it that deeply."

"What particular event in 1840 interests you?"

It was a natural enough question, but Melinda was aware at once of Robin's slight withdrawal. She was too surprised to define that brief narrowing of the eyelids, and then it was past, and he was answering easily, "Oh, nothing particular, just the period."

When the last guest had left, Melinda opened all the windows to let the fresh sea air sweep out the room. The sun had set below the shimmering rim of the Pacific. The lights of Sausalito, Belvedere, Angel Island, Richmond, Berkeley, and Oakland pricked the vivid blue dusk, and the searchlight on Alcatraz—which means "Island of the Pelicans" in Spanish—drew restless circles on the evening sky.

"Do you like Robin, Mums?" asked Melinda with elaborate casualness.

Mrs. Marshall, who was unscrewing her pearl earrings as she always did the moment a party was over, put them behind a candlestick on the mantle where she wouldn't find them for a month and answered, "Darling, do you think I'd entrust you for a long drive to a man I *didn't* like?"

A remembered whisper brushed Melinda's ear: *To trust a stranger is to walk a dark road without a lantern.* But she resolutely shut her mind to it, and, flying across the room, she swept her mother off her feet in a grateful hug.

CHAPTER SIX

The Man in the White Mask

THE following morning Melinda awoke to her mother's voice saying: "Lindy lamb, time to get up. Petunia says that we have to eat up the pancake flour. *Do* you remember where I put my pearl earrings last night?"

Melinda blinked. There were times when Mums talked like a spool of confetti. She unwound whatever came into her head, tore off the sentence, and tossed it to the nearest listener. Melinda never forgot the day when they were shopping after school and they'd run into Mr. Hoskins, the science teacher. Melinda had been in great awe of Mr. Hoskins then. Fervently hoping that Mums would make one of her gracious, just-right remarks, Melinda heard her say: "Dear Mr. Hoskins, you're rocks and trees and things, aren't you? I'm looking for some pajamas with pink hearts for my husband's birthday. I want to surprise him. Have you seen any? Lindy tells me you're simply bloodcurdling with frogs."

Mr. Hoskins hadn't been the same for a week afterward.

"They're downstairs on the mantel, Mums, behind the candlestick," said Melinda, fishing for her slippers.

Her mother floated across the room in a cloud of chiffon negligee. "*Candlestick?* Whatever was I thinking of?" She sighed. "You know, it was your father's idea starting at nine, not mine. I haven't even begun to pack yet."

Melinda remembered Daddy's remark that his wife never thought about having the trunks brought down from the attic until she heard the train whistle. She blew a kiss at her beautiful, unpredictable mother as she went down to breakfast.

She found her father sitting alone at the table in front of a pile of hot cakes. "Welcome to the great pancake panic," he greeted her. "Oh, Petunia, not *more?*" he groaned as another fragrant stack appeared.

"Yassir. And there's bacon and eggs comin' up, too. Takin' eggs for a loppity long ride don't improve their disposition."

Melinda reached for the maple syrup. "Where's Honey Rose?"

"She finished a minute ago. And your mother has forgotten all about breakfast. Listen."

They could hear Mrs. Marshall's slippers on the floor above them, pit-patting faster and faster as the hands of the clock swung toward nine. It was the crescendo known as Keep-Out-of-the-Way-Everybody-Mums-Is-Packing.

Father and daughter exchanged a grin.

As soon as she finished, Melinda hurried into the living room to see if her mother had found her pearl earrings behind the candlestick.

She hadn't.

Melinda had just started upstairs with them when there was the sound of a jet plane making a three-point landing in front of the house.

As she dashed down again to open the door, Robin pressed the bell. "Happy Thursday, Melinda!" His hands were strong and eager as he reached for both of hers. In white officer's shorts and a blue shirt open at the throat with a Paisley scarf tucked into it he looked as tanned and English as a Bermuda travel poster.

"I'm all ready," announced Melinda. "And Mums says we don't have to wait for them."

"Your obedient servant, ma'am."

He carried out Melinda's suitcase and several boxes while she followed with the riding boots. After the last trip he turned to her. "You get into the front seat so I can pack things around you. Otherwise I might get halfway to the moon and find that I'd left my most important charge behind!"

Melinda obeyed, at the same time informing him that it wasn't the moon they were headed for, but the *Valley* of the Moon.

"What's the difference? It's all one moon. Mind your head. I think there's just room for these tennis rackets behind you. No? Then you'll have to hold them, my girl. Oh, there is room? I thought so." He grinned at her, then went around to the other side and folded himself into the driver's seat.

Just as he started the engine, Melinda suddenly wailed: "Oh, Robin, wait! I haven't said good-by to the family."

He turned to look at her. He couldn't see much except a nutmeg-freckled nose, golden hair, and a pair of beseeching eyes above a lapful of coats and cameras and jars of Petunia's peach-and-almond jam. "Look here, Miss Marshall," he said sternly, "you're making history; you're going to the moon. No time for social amenities. You don't think Columbus unpacked everything to go and say good-by to the family, do you?"

Melinda's eyes were so crinkled up with laughter that she didn't even notice Honey Rose until she came tripping across the sidewalk to see them off. The Southern girl soon made it so obvious that she wished she were going with them that Melinda couldn't resist saying, "Lucky you, you'll be so comfortable in that nice big Buick," at which Honey Rose gave her a look that nearly blistered Lightnin' Bug's yellow paint.

A minute later Mr. and Mrs. Marshall also came out to say good-by. "You'll probably get there first, Lindy," said Mr. Marshall. "Tell Doña Ysabel I'm bringing the tire. And, Robin"—he surveyed Lightnin' Bug dubiously—"for heaven's sake drive carefully. That's our only daughter you've got aboard."

Robin inclined his head. "I assure you that I shall take every precaution, sir. This is also my only car."

He started the engine again and with a supersonic whoosh Lightnin' Bug roared off down the street.

Mr. Marshall gazed after it. "Perhaps our neighbors hadn't planned to sleep late this morning, anyway," he murmured to his wife.

The little MG turned the corner and then zoomed down the hill. The Bay was peacock blue in the sun; a meringue of clouds topped the East Bay hills; the bell tower of the University of California punctuated Berkeley like an exclamation point.

Melinda gave a small kitten stretch of delight. If anyone had told her yesterday that she would be setting off for the ranch this morning in a crazy, wonderful car with a handsome young Englishman . . .

"Do you always glow like this at half-past nine on Thursday mornings?" inquired Robin as they approached the Golden Gate Bridge.

Melinda turned pink. She hadn't realized that it *showed*. "It's ... it's a glowy sort of day, don't you think?"

"The glowiest day I've known," agreed Robin, "since yesterday!"

Something about the way he said it made Melinda even pinker.

Through the tollgate—where the friendly guard wished them a nice day—and then they were setting out across the longest single-span bridge in the world. Melinda leaned back, watching the cables soar to the top of the 750-foot scarlet towers like the flight of a bird captured in steel.

"But, Melinda," exclaimed Robin, "it's *red!* I thought it would be golden!"

Melinda chuckled as the offshore wind plucked a curl from under her scarf. "Sorry, Robin, but the Golden Gate was here long before 1937 when the bridge was built." She pointed to their left where two points of land curved like welcoming hands to form the entrance to the Bay. "That is the real Golden Gate. Of course it's not golden, either, but Frémont, who named it over a hundred years ago, was thinking of the Golden Horn of Constantinople. He said that someday this harbor would rival that one. And then just a year or two after he named it ... gold was discovered here and all the world that came clamoring to the Gold Rush sailed in through the Golden Gate!"

"Hmmmm, I guess John Charles Frémont was more successful as a prophet than he was as a presidential candidate."

Melinda turned in surprise. "How do you know about Frémont?"

"Oh, he's the kind of man I admire," Robin told her enthusiastically. "Everything he did was an adventure: map-ping the Oregon Trail, governor of California, general in the Civil War, leader in the Bear Flag Revolt, first man to run for president on the Republican ticket . . . he was a real pioneer."

As he spoke, Melinda thought of the valiant little island Robin himself came from, with its traditions of Drake and Livingston and Scott of the Antarctic. It had never occurred to her before, but with their courage and courtesy, honor and humor—and just a touch of swashbuckling—they were indeed kinsmen to the pioneers of the early West.

They reached the end of the bridge. "Oh, Robin," exclaimed Melinda. "Look around. Isn't that beautiful?"

"In the middle of a six-lane highway," replied Robin, "and remembering your father's caution that I have his only daughter aboard. I will *not* look around. What is it?"

"Sorry," said Melinda in a small voice. "It's just that Telegraph Hill looks so lovely with the sun on it."

"Why is it called Telegraph Hill?" Robin wanted to know. "Does Western Union own it?"

Melinda giggled. "They probably wish they did! No, in the early days there was a sort of windmill on that hill with movable wooden arms. The way the arms were placed 'telegraphed' to the town what sort of ship was entering the harbor. Everybody knew the code, and the whole city would leave whatever it was doing and rush down to the wharf to welcome it. A ship was their lifeline. It brought everything from mail to clean laundry."

"*Laundry?*" repeated Robin.

She nodded. "At the time of the Gold Rush, there was a shortage of fresh water in San Francisco. Drinking water was brought over in rowboats from the springs in Sausalito, but it was too precious to wash in. So people sent their laundry out by sailing vessel to Hawaii or Canton. It came back by the next ship."

"So that's it," announced Robin grimly. "My laundry in Oxford must have been sending *my* shirts around the Horn!"

In a minute the road dipped through a cleft in the hills and they came out at water level below the cliff-clinging artists' colony of Sausalito. Then, as they drove on toward San Rafael, they left the sea behind them and the temperature climbed into the nineties. Soon the green steepness of the Bay Area gave way to toasted golden-brown hills folding into each other.

"Don't the hills look like muffins just out of the oven?" asked Melinda.

"And someboy's forgotten to turn the oven off!" answered Robin, mopping his forehead.

Their route took them through Sonoma where the Bear Flag was raised in 1846, proclaiming California an independent republic. The Republic lasted only a month, but the Bear Flag still flies over all state buildings in California.

At Glen Ellen they turned off onto a dirt road. It was hot and dusty, but the valley was thick with California oaks, madrone, laurel, toyon, and twisted manzanitas with their flame-red bark. As they wound along the narrow track, the air was heavy with the motionless stillness of noon. The only sounds were cicadas drilling a hole in the heat with their high-pitched buzz, and an occasional swarm of gnats spinning across the road like a phantom top.

Lightnin' Bug puffed protestingly as the road dipped down to the dry bed of a stream. "Come on, old girl," Robin clucked encouragingly. "Think of King Arthur, think of the Light Brigade, think of Hilary climbing Everest. You can do it, too."

"It's only another mile," added Melinda.

They rattled across the dip, with the MG making more and more ominous noises.

"What's the matter, buggy?" asked Robin. "This is nothing. Don't you remember the Porlock Hill in Devon? You skimmed up that like a . . . ."

But apparently remembering the Porlock Hill in Devon was the last straw for Lightnin' Bug. With a final hiccough, the car expired.

"What the—" exclaimed Robin as they rolled back a few feet to the bottom of the stream bed and rocked to a stop. The air around them quivered in waves of heat like thick glass, and a bluejay dived between the trees, a bright stroke of blue against the dusty leaves.

"Have we run out of gas?" asked Melinda.

"I just filled the petrol tank before we left." Getting out of the car, Robin poked at the engine.

Suddenly a cicada began its metallic shrilling from a branch above him. Robin jumped. "Goodness, I thought I'd done that!" Returning to Melinda, he announced, "It's the petrol, all right, I mean gas! There must be a leak. Where's the nearest service station?"

"Miles away. But we're only a short distance from the ranch now and Daddy keeps a can of gas in the garage for emergencies."

"Righto. I'm a fast walker; I'll be back in half an hour. You just sit here and . . . ."

"Is that so?" retorted Melinda sweetly. She was already half out of the car. "Thank you. I've leaned against your tennis racket long enough. My back feels like a Swiss steak."

Despite the heat it wasn't an unpleasant walk. They said

little. Robin never found silence embarrassing or boring. When he had something to say, he said it, but his personality was too vital, too sure of itself, to be made self-conscious by a companionable quietness. Melinda knew that he was paying her the compliment of being at ease with her and not feeling that he must frost over a mere acquaintanceship with the whipped cream of chatter. In turn she tried to undo her old habit of rushing to fill every pause in a conversation.

They had gone about a quarter of the way when Melinda suddenly realized that she had left her handbag lying on the seat of the car, and the MG was open.

"Oh, Robin, I've got to run back. I left my purse in the car."

"Won't it be safe there? We're miles from anywhere."

"I know. But it's got the family keys in it and . . . and my whole month's allowance!" Her voice was contrite. "I'm awfully sorry."

Robin tried to look masculinely superior and annoyed, but his blue eyes held a giveaway twinkle. "How like a woman! Come on, back we go."

His strides ate up the road; Melinda had to run to keep up with him. It was only a few minutes when they again caught a flash of yellow in the gully.

"I'll run ahead. I know just where I left it." Without waiting for him, Melinda took off, sandals skimming over the gravel.

She turned a corner where the road curved around an oak. Once past its screen of low-hanging branches she could see the little MG clearly, not fifty feet away.

And there was a man bending over it!

At the sound of her footsteps he jerked upright. For one

instant of time he stood there, motionless as a startled animal. Then he turned and disappeared like a streak through the underbrush. He was wearing a broad-brimmed canvas hat and a dirty raincoat.

But on the face was a white mask with two holes cut for the eyes.

"Robin!" cried Melinda.

CHAPTER SEVEN

Birthday Present

THE next second Robin was beside her. "Melinda, what is it?"

"There was ... there was somebody at the car. A man. He was bending over the back seat. He fled when he saw me."

Grabbing her hand, Robin was already running down the slope. When they reached the car, he searched it thoroughly. "Nothing's missing that I can see," he announced at last. "Even your purse is right there on the seat. We must have surprised him. What did he look like?"

In a shaky voice Melinda described the raincoat, the white blob of a face.

"You mean a *mask?*" Robin frowned.

"I ... I guess so."

"I wonder what he was looking for. It must have been a tramp. But why the mask?" He paused.

Before he could go on, the noontide stillness was suddenly shattered by a loud honk. Swinging around the bend, a car pulled up behind Lightnin' Bug.

They both jumped. Then, when they saw Mr. and Mrs. Marshall, Honey Rose and Petunia, they grinned apologetically.

"Sorry, sir, but we've run out of petrol," called Robin.

"Don't worry," answered Mr. Marshall. "I have an extra gallon here."

Melinda thought that Honey Rose and Mums looked a little wilted, but Petunia was sitting bolt upright with her favorite saucepan on her lap and a beret of gold sequins on her head. She looked like a high priestess bringing news from the oracle.

Mr. Marshall helped Robin pour in the gas. Then he remarked with a sigh to a nearby manzanita bush: "Parents *do* have their uses."

"Yes, thank you, Daddy," called Melinda sweetly as her father trudged back to the Buick. Slipping into the MG's front seat, she said softly to Robin, "Are . . . are we going to tell them?"

"Of course," replied Robin in surprise. "And we must let the police know, too."

Melinda said nothing. She was thinking: *This is the second time I've been with Robin, and this is the second time something . . . dangerous . . . has happened. Is this what the whisper meant by "trusting a stranger"?*

It was less than ten minutes later when they crested a rise and came out of the trees. And with that sudden sweep of brown hills on either side it was as though portals had swung wide before them.

Robin slowed the car. "I say," he murmured.

Below them lay El Rancho de la Colina de Oro, Ranch of the Golden Hill. The estate had been in Mrs. Marshall's family for more than a hundred and fifty years. Many an oxcart filled with flounce-skirted and fringe-shawled guests on their way to a *merienda* had creaked down this road in the 1840's. Many a dashing ranchero, riding over from a neighboring estate in glove-tight riding breeches, white ruffled shirt, black velvet bolero, and broad-brimmed black hat with a cord under the chin, had tied up his pinto at that horse rail, sunshine picking out the gay hemp embroidery and goat-hair fringe on his carved leather saddle.

Melinda had read treasured family letters of fiestas at Colina de Oro with a hundred guests fed and housed for a week. Her godmother, Doña Ysabel, would translate the ornate Spanish writing for her and then open the great Mexican leather and wood trunks so that she could browse among pleated scarlet petticoats, silk shawls, tall tortoise-shell combs, and shimmering lace mantillas. In another box were the brocades, faded plumes, tiny pointed slippers, and sequin-sprinkled fans which had come from France in the 1850's in Felix Verdier's clipper ship, the *Ville de Paris*. This was the forerunner of San Francisco's present-day department store, the City of Paris.

Robin Sutherland, looking down on the valley, saw only a stanchly built house around an open patio. The four-foot-thick walls of adobe were pierced by small, wide-silled windows—originally without glass—shadowed by deep eaves. The roof was the traditional red tile for protection against flaming Indian arrows. For shade there were a cluster of feather-fingered eucalyptus and one great old pepper tree spangled with tiny berries the shiny pink of rose quartz.

"It's like a painting out of another century," said Robin softly. "Tell me its story, Melinda. Was gold really found here?"

She shook her head. "Not that kind of gold. But in the spring the hill is a sweep of California poppies. When my great-great—I always forget how many *greats!*—grandfather received this land in grant from the Mexican governor, he had to persuade his gentle, high-born Spanish bride to come with him into the wilderness of Alta California. He didn't dare tell her about the heat and the dense forest to be cleared and the Indians and the wild animals. So he told her, instead, about the crystal springs which never dry up, and the nearness of the stars on a summer night, and the acres of golden poppies in April. When he came to the poppies, so the family story goes, his bride broke down and said 'I come!' So of course the new rancho was named Colina de Oro, Golden Hill."

Robin was pulling up in front of the house. The Buick parked beside them, and Honey Rose got out, smoothing her skirt. "Now wouldn't a nice tall glass of iced tea taste grand right this minute?" she remarked hopefully to no one in particular.

"No use your now-wouldn'ting me, chile, Ah've got work to do," replied Petunia firmly as Mr. Marshall unlocked the front door.

The door was the original one, a massive slab of wood

carved in the pattern called River of Life, with four wavy panels symbolizing the Four Gospels.

The house was dark after the noonday glare and the low, wide, whitewashed rooms were cool as a cave. One wall of the living room had been cleaned of paint to reveal the original Mexican frescoes, muted to the colors of an antique rug. Robin and Melinda went down a hall which had originally been the rancho's *corredor*, an outdoor arcade copied from Spanish convents, onto which all the rooms opened. When new rooms were later added to Colina de Oro, the *corredor* was enclosed and became the long central hall. Robin caught a glimpse of cedar roof beams, antique Spanish-Mexican furniture interspersed with comfortable modern armchairs, a dark carved-wood Madonna in a niche, the splash of geraniums in a pottery bowl, fat creamy candles in tin sconces, and a scalloped tin chandelier ... and then Melinda opened a door at the end, and Robin found himself in the most twentieth century of kitchens.

He put down the crate of preserves he was carrying and stared at the gleaming freezer, the dishwasher, the mixer under its plastic tent. "I can't get over American kitchens. Do you really *use* all these things, or do you just keep them to impress visiting Englishmen?"

"Of course we use them. So will you when we have the barbecue tomorrow. We all have to pitch in and help Petunia."

While Melinda went out to put the preserves in the pantry, Robin gazed respectfully at the huge refrigerator. "I wonder what the early settlers would have thought of this?"

There was a rich chuckle in the doorway behind him.

"Probably just what you are thinking, señor; have we surely enough to feed a hundred people?"

Robin turned quickly. "I beg your pard..." He stopped, blinking. Was that figure framed in the doorway *real?* Or was it a ghost, a shadow cast by the long, candlelighted past of Golden Hill?

The woman who stood straight as a queen on the threshold was old, so old that she had long ago entered that more gentle world where the years only curtsied as they passed and did not touch her. Her skin was transparent as faded petals; her long fingers were freighted with rings; above the fine-boned face was piled a cloud of smoke-gray hair. Her dress was black velvet over a pleated taffeta petticoat, and the square of lace about her shoulders was pinned with a blaze of garnets. A faint scent of damask roses floated into the room before her.

"Welcome to El Rancho de la Colina de Oro, señor." She spoke with the lilt of a Spanish accent. *"Está usted en su casa—* you are in your own home. I suppose Melinda forgot to say that as you crossed the threshold."

Before Robin could reply, Melinda came back from the pantry. The instant she saw the figure in the doorway, she flew across the kitchen. Robin expected the vision in black to snap like a fragile twig under that windmill hug, but she seemed to like it.

Then Melinda was drawing him forward. "Doña Ysabel, may I present Robin Sutherland? Robin, this is my godmother and"—her voice softened—"my dearest friend!"

Doña Ysabel held out her hand. With a courtly bow Robin brushed it with his lips. Melinda felt a little rush of pride. Robin had known the one thing to do that would please Doña Ysabel, and he had done it so easily, so unaffectedly. Doña

Ysabel's eyes glowed in surprise. "So there *are* some who re-member the old courtesies. And as the Spanish say, courtesies are little candles on the staircase of life." She turned to Melinda. "Is that everything, dear?"

"There's one more load, Doña Ysabel, and Daddy's got the tractor tire. If you'll excuse us . . ."

Out of earshot of the kitchen Robin murmured, "What a remarkable woman!"

Melinda nodded as they reached the car. "She was born here and she hasn't left the ranch in fifty years. But she has promised to come down to San Francisco for my debut in December."

"Who takes care of her?"

Melinda looked startled. "Takes care of *her?* She takes care of the ranch. She runs it for us."

"By Jove!" There was awe in Robin's voice. Then he added, "By the way, Melinda, we must tell your father about the . . . the tramp right away."

Her smile faded. For a moment the joy she felt to be "home" had pushed the man in the mask from her mind. But now, with a sober nod, she went with Robin to the library where her father was unwrapping some books.

Mr. Marshall listened to their story with deepening concern. When they had finished, he dialed the sheriff at once. After he hung up, he reported, "They're going to search the woods. Although I suppose he's miles away by now."

"We thought it might be . . . a tramp, sir," suggested Robin.

A low, vibrant voice from the doorway answered him. "It was not a tramp."

They all turned as Doña Ysabel came in. Mr. Marshall said swiftly, "How do you know, Ysabel?"

The Spanish dowager crossed the room to a high-backed chair and sat down with regal deliberateness. "Every tramp in the West knows that he can get a free meal and a night's lodging at Colina de Oro, Charles. He would not need to rummage in parked cars. *And hoboes do not wear masks*."

Mr. Marshall nodded. He hesitated for a moment, then said to Melinda, "I don't think we need to mention this to your mother or Honey Rose. If they happen to see the sheriff, well, he's hunting for a strayed horse. No sense in scaring them. But I think I'll have a talk with Miguel, ask him if he's seen any strangers around the ranch lately."

There was a snort from the high-backed chair. "To Miguel the truth is only a young wistaria vine to be twisted whichever way casts the most flattering shade on Miguel."

"You think I don't know that?" demanded Mr. Marshall. "Miguel is the slipperiest, shiftiest, laziest foreman who has ever grown fat off of Colina de Oro. I've told you a thousand times to fire him, Ysabel."

"*Sí, sí!*" Doñ Ysabel lifted her hand. "But he has the touch of an angel with the horses. Some people are born with the gift of *simpatía* for animals. It has nothing whatever to do with their morals," she finished dryly.

Before Mr. Marshall could reply, there was a light tap at the door. "Melinda," came Honey Rose's voice, "Petunia says please will you come help her with luncheon; it's nearly ready."

"Coming!" Melinda hurried to the door.

As she went out, Honey Rose came in. "Am I interrupting?"

With a preoccupied expression, Mr. Marshall said, "I'm going to put the car away."

"Would you like me to move Lightnin' Bug, too, sir?" Robin started after him.

"Thanks, Robin, but it won't be necessary."

Honey Rose touched Robin's arm. "Don't go!" She fluttered her raven's-wing lashes at him. "Unless—unless you're afraid of me, Robin?"

There was a scornful rustle of black taffeta rising from the high-backed chair. "If he knows what's good for him, he will be," remarked Doña Ysabel.

Laughing, Robin sprang to open the door for her. Just as she passed him, her right eyelid flickered in his direction.

Robin turned back into the room. "Do I gather that Doña Ysabel doesn't exactly approve of you?" he asked Honey Rose mischievously.

"Oh, she doesn't understand me." Honey Rose pouted. "In her day, everything was fans and sighs and serenades. Thank heaven, we're more natural and frank nowadays."

"A pity, perhaps," murmured Robin. "No one would look lovelier than you behind a black lace fan!"

Honey Rose looked up at him with a little cry of delight. "Why, Robin Sutherland, you're human, after all! I was just about to give up."

He grinned at her. "And besides, fluttering a fan would give your eyelashes a rest."

With a swoop, she grabbed a geranium and threw it at him.

He ducked, laughing. "Come on, let's help with luncheon. I'm starved!"

After ham sandwiches, lemonade, and a big bowl of green salad, they sat around the patio while Doña Ysabel told Robin some of Colina de Oro's history, Mrs. Marshall and Melinda went over the guest list for the next day, and Mr. Marshall read the paper. No one seemed particularly anxious to leave the lazy peace of the patio and start in on any of the jobs which they kept telling each other had to be done right away.

It was nearly four o'clock before they all went into the house, Melinda to help Petunia frost cupcakes for tomorrow. Mr. Marshall and Robin disappeared into the library for a few minutes, and then Robin returned to the kitchen. It wasn't long before he made an opportunity to help Melinda carry a tray of newly frosted cakes out to the pantry.

The pantry had been the original cool room of the ranch. It was tile-floored, whitewashed, and even in midsummer cool enough to keep butter firm.

As soon as the door shut behind them, Robin said: "The sheriff just phoned. He didn't find anyone. But about a quarter of a mile from the gully a car had been parked among the trees."

"Then it *wasn't* a tramp," whispered Melinda.

"He must have followed us until we ran out of petrol." Absently Robin helped himself to a cupcake.

"But how did he know that we were going to run out of pet . . . gas?"

"He could have siphoned it out. Lightnin' Bug was in a public parking lot while I had breakfast this morning." He licked thoughtfully at the frosting. "The sheriff thinks the mask shows that the man was a professional thief."

"But he didn't take my purse," protested Melinda. "What was he *after*? What did he think was in the car to go to all that trouble?"

Robin shook his head. "Maybe he got it mixed up with another MG."

"What's you-all doin' with mah cakes?" demanded Petunia's suspicious voice from the doorway.

Robin turned. "Just seeing that Melinda doesn't eat them all up!" he replied airily.

"Dat so?" retorted Petunia. "Then what's dat frosting doin' on *your* chin?"

As day folded into dusk, the air cooled, the great pepper tree etched a tracery of black lace against the western sky, and through the open windows came the hundred noises of a summer night, rustles, cheeps, and the French accent of crickets trilling their r's.

At bedtime that night Melinda turned out her light, then went to the window to let the peace and stillness of the sleeping Valley of the Moon steal over her. This was a ritual every time she returned to Colina de Oro, this deep, wordless exchange in the dark between herself and the land that was her heritage. Her room overlooked the hillside and the stables, with the loft above them where Miguel lived. Through the silence she heard a whinny. That would be Bess or Star, the work horses; or Miss Midnight, Daddy's magnificent black five-gaited mare.

Melinda drew a long, contented breath. Home again! and then knelt to say her prayers at the open window before climbing into bed.

Her seventeenth birthday began, as had the sixteen others, with a kiss and her mother's voice saying, "Happy birthday, Lindy lamb. Blueberry muffins for breakfast!"

She opened her eyes. Mrs. Marshall was already dressed and there was an excited twinkle in her expression.

Melinda bounced out of bed. "I'll be ready in five secs!"

Pulling on black denim jeans and a white cotton blouse, she ran a brush through her hair until it gleamed like a new penny in the rain, and then hurried out to the patio.

There she found both breakfast and the family waiting. As she appeared in the doorway, Robin led the others in "Happy Birthday to You!"

She stopped on the threshold, overcome with shyness as they all crowded around her with hugs and spanks. The table was piled with packages, and she could smell the butteriness of blueberry muffins.

She had just managed to sit down at the table at last when Petunia came out, her slice-of-watermelon smile wider than ever. "There's somebody at the door, chile. It's for you."

"For me?" Even though this was her birthday, Melinda was surprised. Up here in the country, who could it be so early? She glanced around the table, but everybody was being suddenly very busy with breakfast. If she'd stopped to think, she would have noticed that even Honey Rose was reaching quickly for a blueberry muffin dripping with butter, an event so earth-shaking that she ought to have been warned then and there.

But she only slipped from her chair with an "Excuse me, I'll be right back."

Hurrying down the long hall, she saw that Petunia had let the heavy front door close again after answering it. Gritting her teeth, she wrestled with the ancient hand-forged latch. No use ever suggesting that Mums and Daddy replace it with a modern one. Antiquarians came from all over the West to exclaim in rapture over its rare design. Melinda just wished they had to *open* it once in a while.

But the great door swung wide before her at last.

She blinked in surprise. There was no one there.

Shading her eyes against the sun, she stepped out onto the porch.

"Happy birthday, señorita."

She looked around. And felt as though her heart had stepped on a roller skate.

Miguel was coming across the gravel drive. In one hand he held his best sombrero doffed low in greeting. The other rested light as a caress on the halter of the most beautiful horse Melinda had ever seen.

It was a palomino, the golden horse of the golden West. His coat rippled like silk in the sunlight, his mane and tail were brushed silver, and in perfect match his two forelegs were white to the knee. He had the warm brown eyes, the arching neck, the velvet muzzle of the palomino. His ears pricked when he saw Melinda, and he whinnied softly.

Miguel grinned as he led the shining horse up to the porch. "Silverstockings, he say happy birthday, señorita."

Melinda couldn't move, she couldn't speak. Dimly she was aware that the family had come out and were standing behind her on the porch. "For—for me?" she finally managed, and the voice didn't sound just-seventeen at all.

"For you, Baby," said Mums, and put an arm around her shoulders. "A horse of your very own."

There was something on Melinda's cheek. She lifted a shaky hand to brush it away.

And found that she was crying.

CHAPTER EIGHT

Race at Twilight

AFTER the first numb second of is-this-real? Melinda nearly swept her parents off their feet in an enormous hug. Then, half-laughing, half-crying, she dashed across the drive to Silverstockings.

As she ran her hand over the springing arch of his mane, her cheek pressed to his white blaze, the palomino nibbled at the golden hair tickling his nose. But when her fingers found the little velvety spots behind his ears and began stroking them gently, Silverstockings closed his eyes and made a noise in his throat astonishingly like purring.

Meanwhile Robin, looking on, found himself watching the Mexican foreman. Doña Ysabel had been brave indeed to hire such a sinister-looking hombre. Heavy black brows and deep shadows beneath his eyes formed a peculiar dark stripe across Miguel's face like a bandit's mask, out of which glinted small yellow-green eyes that constantly slithered over and around whatever he was looking at. The mouth was set in a shifty smile; to Robin he looked like a thoroughly unpleasant character.

"But see him with the horse," murmured a soft voice in his ear. Robin turned to find Doña Ysabel beside him. She chuckled. "Probably as long as Miguel is at the ranch none of us are quite safe in our beds . . . but the horses have a friend."

"I see what you mean," he agreed, observing the gentling hand on Silverstockings' flank, the whispered Spanish endearment.

Farther down the drive, Mr. Marshall was taking movies. Mrs. Marshall was telling him how. And Petunia looked on from the safety of the front door. Only Honey Rose seemed to be left out of things.

With quick thoughtfulness Robin turned to her. "Do you ride, Honey Rose?"

She shook her head. "I had polio as a child. My knees won't grip." She said it matter-of-factly, but for the first time Robin caught a glimpse, under the glamour, of a courageous girl who held her head high. With a new respect he smiled at her but only said lightly: "You know, Honey Rose, to an Englishman breakfast is a solemn occasion not to be slighted like this. Do you suppose those blueberry muffins are still warm?"

At once Honey Rose was all come-hither Southern belle again. "Shall we go and see, suh?"

Robin called across the drive to Melinda: "Those of us who didn't get palominos for our birthday are going in to drown our sorrows in blueberry muffins!"

Melinda laughed. "I'll come with you." Planting a last farewell-for-ten-minutes kiss on Silverstockings' velvet nose before Miguel led him back to the stables, she went inside with her family, one arm around Mums' shoulders.

At the table she opened the rest of her presents. A sparkly evening bag from Mums; a lavish-with-lace "bestest" slip from Honey Rose; a pair of silver horseshoe cuff links for her riding shirts from Daddy. At last there were only two boxes left, both white, both preciously tiny.

As Melinda opened the first one, she gasped with joy. Against the faded velvet of an old jewel box glowed an enamel cross on a platinum chain. The enamel was the opalescent rose of a hummingbird's throat.

"Oh, Doña Ysabel, the one I've always loved!" She flew around the table to envelop her godmother in a huge hug.

Doña Ysabel's eyes misted for a moment. "That jewel was a wedding gift from the King of Spain to the bride who was the first mistress of Colina de Oro. Remember her when you wear it, child; and may the Holy Angels grant you her gaiety, her compassion, her shining courage." She brushed a kiss against Melinda's cheek.

Melinda swallowed hard. "I will," she promised.

The last box of all was tied with plain white ribbon and there was no card with it.

"I wonder who ..." Melinda murmured as she untied it. The next moment her eyes were sudden stars. "Oh, *Robin!*"

It was a little gold lion for her charm bracelet.

"The B-B-British lion," explained Robin, very pink under his tan, "so you won't forget a B-B-British friend."

Impulsively Melinda reached out her hand across the table. "I'll never forget, Robin. Thank you will all my heart."

For a second his fingers tightened over hers.

Like all special once-a-year days this one flew past on swallow's wings. Melinda had barely folded away the wrappings, changed to a crisp cotton sundress, and flown up the hill to the stables to make sure that nothing had happened to Silverstockings in the last five minutes, when the first guests began to arrive for the birthday barbecue.

It was a wonderful party, with friends from all over Northern California. The governor came from Sacramento; Melinda's school friends piled out of a chartered bus hung with a big streamer HAPPY BIRTHDAY, LINDY! The Baron de Palafox drove up in his Citroën DS 19 with its special manual controls, wishing Melinda "Many happy ... how do you say ... *comebacks* of the day."

Ever since early morning barbecuing chicken and spareribs had been wafting tantalizing smells over the ranch. At two o'clock they were done. After tennis or a swim or just lazing, the guests lined up, then took their plates to lawn chairs.

Robin found himself sitting on the low stone rim around the base of the pepper tree with Honey Rose beside him. Melinda was busy passing hot garlic French bread. Across the patio, enthroned in a peacock rattan chair, Doña Ysabel was holding court.

"Is she a widow?" Robin asked Honey Rose.

"You mean all that black? No, Doña Ysabel never married. She was engaged to an Englishman who was killed out in India. She has worn black for him since she was nineteen."

"I wonder how many girls would do that nowadays," mused Robin. "Remain faithful unto death, I mean."

"Well, *I* wouldn't," stated Honey Rose. "Living in a memory like that is—is morbid."

Robin looked at her thoughtfully. "No, I don't imagine you would." He smiled.

When the sun had sloped below the hill, Mr. Marshall brought out the phonograph for dancing in the patio. As soon as the music started, Robin was not surprised to find Honey Rose gracefully in his way.

He found her a good dancer, although he wished she

wouldn't go so limp against him. He was just wondering how to ask her please to bear up on her own, as it had been a long day for him, too, when the music came to an end.

"Mmmm, that was dreamy," she breathed.

Mr. Marshall, crossing the patio, murmured as he passed Robin, "Watch out, my boy, the Southern belle is ringing for you!"

Robin grinned and then went to find Melinda.

"Oh, Robin, she excused herself to go and change. She wants a ride on her birthday present before it gets dark," Mrs. Marshall called to him. In spite of being a gay hostess all day with the temperature in the nineties, she still looked as cool and fresh as a sprig of mint. "Have you any riding things with you?"

"Just dungarees, I'm afraid."

"They're all right. My husband can lend you some western boots. Melinda would like to have you go with her. You do ride, don't you, Robin?"

"Yes, Mrs. Marshall, I do." Knowing British understatement, Mrs. Marshall decided that he probably had a shelf full of silver trophies at home, which happened to be true. "By the way, which horse do I take?"

"My husband's, Miss Midnight. You don't know how privileged you are, Robin. It's as though Mr. Cunard suggested that you take the *Queen Mary* for a trial spin all by yourself!"

With this heady information, Robin changed, and a minute later went in search of Melinda. She was waiting for him near the kitchen door.

"How do the boots feel?"

"Tickety-boo, if I don't fall flat on my face with these high cowboy heels!"

"They're so that your foot won't slip through the stirrup if you're thrown, dragging you," she told him as they started up the hill toward the stables. "And the pointed toes help a cowboy to find the stirrup in a hurry."

Although the sun had dropped behind the ridge of hills around the ranch, the twilight sky was still bright with a pearly ripple of clouds like the iridescent inside of an abalone shell.

The stables were cool and smelled of hay and saddle soap as Melinda and Robin went in. Silverstockings was already saddled and waiting. He greeted Melinda with an affectionate nuzzle.

Miguel was tightening the cinch on Miss Midnight. He didn't look up as they approached, but Robin was conscious of a pair of yellow eyes watching critically as he mounted.

Melinda unsnapped the rope from the palomino's bridle and swung into the saddle. As they rode out through the wide stable doors, Miguel gave a grunt of admiration at the way Robin controlled the prancing black mare.

They walked the horses up the hill toward the grazing range. Silverstockings held his head proudly, like a Spanish hidalgo. His ears pricked at every cricket chirp or flutter of quail in the underbrush. Occasionally he would turn and survey Miss Midnight, her slim, black-stockinged legs arching beside him. He gave her cheek a nudge and the little mare rolled coquettish eyes at him.

"Is Miss Midnight a Southern horse?" asked Robin suddenly.

Melinda looked surprised. "Why, yes. Daddy got her in Tennessee. How did you know?"

"I'm getting so that I can recognize the signs," he replied

with a straight face as Miss Midnight fluttered her long black eyelashes at Silverstockings.

Melinda giggled.

The track had been winding upward. Now they reached the crest; below them acres of rolling pasture dipped away to the horizon. Down the center curved a silver stream; along its banks the willows trailed green fingers in the water, and a clump of California oaks flung their long, black shadows over the grass. Cattle were grazing in the meadows; somewhere across the valley a dog barked.

Robin drew a deep breath. "I wish I could wrap up these peaceful acres and post them home with a note: *This is the real California*. Not Hollywood or supermarkets or freeways, but the slope of sun-warmed fields and a murmur of wind through the pepper trees at twilight." He looked over at Melinda. "And a golden girl on a golden horse," he added softly. "When I'm back in England and the rain is dripping from the eaves and the evening is long and cold and l-l-lonely, this is the picture I'll remember."

It was a long speech for Robin, and Melinda's cheeks were glowing. She lowered her eyes, curling a strand of Silverstockings' mane over her finger. "To—to me it's heaven, too," she answered with a little catch in her breath. Then she went on hastily, "Do you know that that's what the word *California* means?"

"Heaven?" repeated Robin.

She nodded. "Back in the fifteenth century a Spanish novelist named Montalvo wrote a book called—called"—her forehead puckered—"oh, yes, *Las Sergas de Esplandián*, The Exploits of Esplandián. It was a novel about an imaginary country named California lying at the right hand of the Indies, 'very close to paradise'!"

Robin looked surprised. "You mean that California was named for a place in a *book?* I say, as a hopeful author, that's encouraging!"

"Yes, you see the Spaniards set out to find a northwest passage to the Orient and the legendary Seven Cities of Cibola. Instead, they arrived here. At first they thought this new country was the land of the Amazons because the Indians were so tall and handsome. But then one of Cortés' lieutenants, Francisco de Ulloa, decided that it looked just like that paradise Montalvo had talked about in his novel. So he said that what they had really found was the fabled *California!*"

While she spoke they had been walking their horses down toward the ribbon of stream. In the dusk Melinda's hair was just the color of Silverstockings' shining coat.

But the fading light made Robin glance at his watch. "We've been gone three quarters of an hour, Melinda. Do you think we ought to start back?"

"My, has it been that long?" exclaimed Melinda, then blushed, as she remembered having said those same words when she was with Robin before. She wheeled Silverstockings around, her eyes sparkling with a sudden idea. "There's a grand long stretch up there along the fence. Let's have a real gallop."

"Tallyho!" agreed Robin. "Er . . . English for *heigho, Silver!*" he explained as they pricked heels to their horses.

Miss Midnight shot away with a toss of black mane, but Silverstockings merely arched his tail and his neck, lifted his white stockings, and pranced sideways as though he were in a parade.

"What's he like?" shouted Robin over his shoulder.

"Gorgeous, but I'm afraid he knows it," Melinda called back, trying to get Silverstockings to think more about a real gallop and less about curtsying to an imaginary audience.

The straight track followed a stock fence for more than a mile. At the far end a single towering eucalyptus stood sentinel over the valley.

"I've got an idea," cried Melinda eagerly. "Let's race to the tree. Winner gets an extra slice of birthday cake!"

Robin reined in until he was abreast of her, "Melinda, do you think we ought . . . ."

But she had held up her hand. "One, two"—she dropped it—"THREE!"

Miss Midnight was off like a black arrow, her slim hoofs barely touching the ground. In ten seconds she had put three lengths between herself and an astonished palomino.

Melinda leaned forward in the saddle along Silverstockings' neck. "Are you going to let that little Tar Baby win? Show them what you're made of, Silverstockings. Come on!"

After the first surprise Silverstockings really did seem to realize that there was another horse ahead of him and that he was supposed to do something about it. With a tremendous burst of power which almost unseated Melinda, he struck out.

In a few seconds Robin was aware of thundering hoofs coming up on his right. He glanced around. Silverstockings had shortened the distance between them to a length, half a length. The palomino wore a suddenly businesslike expression on his gay and carefree face. Melinda's hair was flying in the wind, her cheeks pink, her eyes sparkling. Robin had never seen her look prettier.

"Tallyho!" she shouted as she passed him.

There were only another hundred feet to the eucalyptus tree, but somehow Robin did not touch Miss Midnight with his whip. This was one race he didn't mind losing.

The tree came spinning toward them along the dusty track. Silverstockings was a length ahead.

As she passed it, Melinda rose in her stirrups and turned around to wave at Robin. "Hurrah for Silverst . . ."

"*Look out!*" shouted Robin.

On the far side of the thick bole of the tree a page of newspaper was caught on the fence. At that moment a gust of wind plucked it loose and sent it whirling across the track.

The flapping whiteness loomed out of the dusk almost under the feet of the galloping horse.

With a snort of terror Silverstockings reared.

And Melinda went hurtling through the air over his head.

The palomino thundered on down the trail. Behind him he left a crumpled heap under the eucalyptus tree, motionless as a rag doll.

CHAPTER NINE

Night Over Colina de Oro

LEAPING from the saddle, Robin dashed back to Melinda. Desperately he felt for the pulse in her limp wrist. He had been present at spills on the hunting field, he knew first aid, he had a cool head in emergencies. But for the first time in his life he couldn't even think. She was so frighteningly white and still, her hair the only brightness in the dusk.

"Melinda," he whispered, "*Melinda.*"

Hoofs trotted back along the path and Silverstockings nudged his shoulder. "Poor old chap, it wasn't your fault," murmured Robin. "That paper would have scared a stone."

He knew that Melinda should not be moved in case a bone was broken. But he couldn't leave her here; it was almost dark. He had to take the risk of carrying her back to the ranch.

Miss Midnight joined Silverstockings. They stood quietly in the twilight, their shoulders touching.

Robin hooked the reins over his left hand. Then, with infinite gentleness, he stooped and gathered Melinda into his arms. Her head against his shoulder, he straightened carefully, and set his face to the long walk home.

Every few steps he glanced down at her, searching in an agony of hope for the slightest flutter. But her eyes were closed, the tiny veins clear against the paper whiteness of her lids. Robin felt a stab at his heart that startled him. *"Please, dear Lord, please,"* he prayed incoherently.

Then, with a tenderness he had never felt before, he bent down and touched his lips to her forehead.

At the brush of that kiss, like the Sleeping Beauty, Melinda stirred.

Robin stopped still, his eyes fixed on hers, every ounce of his strength willing her back to consciousness. Silverstockings whinnied softly.

And Melinda opened her eyes.

"I won," she said in a matter-of-fact voice.

Joy flooded over Robin in a rush. "Yes, darling, you've won!" he whispered huskily. Then his arms tightened around her. Hardly knowing what he did, he dropped his head and buried his face in her hair. "Dear God, thank you."

That "darling" and the feel of his warm cheek against her forehead brought Melinda fully alive with a throb. "Robin," she murmured hurriedly, astonished at the tumultuous racing of her heart, "I think you'd better put me down."

Gently he lowered her feet to the ground. She leaned against him, weak and dizzy, then turned her head to look at the two horses—Silverstockings was regarding her with great concern— the empty track, a paring of moon.

"What did I hit?" she asked Robin.

"You landed on your shoulder. I was so afraid it was broken." Skilfully he ran his hand from shoulder to wrist. "But I guess it's tickety-boo. Thank heaven you didn't hit your head."

She forced a smile. "I've fallen off so many times that I'm made of rubber!"

"We'll get you right back to the house and call a doctor."

"Oh, no." Her eyes flew wide in alarm. "The family mustn't know I've fallen. They might never let me ride Silverstockings again. They might even take him back." She clung to him imploringly. "Please, Robin, don't tell them!"

His face was grave. "But you might be hurt, Melinda—seriously."

"I'm just shaken a bit. If I don't feel all right tomorrow, I'll tell them myself, honest I will."

He gave in unwillingly.

"And we must mount again," Melinda insisted, "so they won't ask questions."

With many misgivings Robin lifted her into the saddle. "Sure you're all right?"

She nodded down at him. "Fine." She didn't add that her shoulder was throbbing and her fingers so weak she could barely hold the reins.

To Robin's relief, Colina de Oro was just over the next rise. In less than five minutes it lay below them, a teaspoon of lights at the bottom of a bowl of darkness.

Robin made her ride down to the kitchen door and dismount, then grinned at her earnest "You will take care of Silverstockings, won't you, Robin?"

"I'll lay on the gold service for him," he promised. "Now you take care of *yourself!*"

After giving the palomino a special hug "so he won't think I don't love him any longer," Melinda let Robin lead him up to the stables.

In the house she found that the last guests had left. The family were in the kitchen, helping Petunia with the dishes.

"Have a good ride?" They all asked in chorus.

"Wonderful," she answered bravely. Which was really true, because parts of the ride *had* been wonderful—more wonderful than she could ever tell them. "Where's a towel? I'll help dry."

"Certainly not, pet." Honey Rose took the dishcloth out of her hands. "This is your birthday, remember? Nobody dries dishes on their birthday."

"We're almost through," put in Mums. "You run along to bed. You look a little tired, Baby."

For once Melinda didn't need urging. She kissed her parents, thanking them again for every minute of her exciting birthday, and hoping they didn't notice that she wasn't using her left arm to hug with.

Honey Rose went down the hall with her. "Jimmy Carter phoned just after you left. He's coming to lunch tomorrow. He said to tell you he was terribly sorry he couldn't make it today."

Jimmy Carter?

Melinda almost had to think for a moment whom he was. Dear old Jimmy! He was the son of her mother's best friend, she'd grown up with him, he was to be her partner for the Debutante Cotillion in December. Mums thought he was the pussycat's whiskers. It only remained for *her* to think so, too. She drew a deep breath. "That'll be . . . nice," she said.

Honey Rose gave her a quizzical smile. "I wonder if Robin will think so! Good night, pet."

After Honey Rose shut the door, Melinda was suddenly so worn out that she could barely find the strength to dab iodine on her scratches, wash her face, and take two aspirin before collapsing into bed, "limper than cold macaroni," she told herself disgustedly.

She awoke four hours later to find the crescent moon caught in her organdy curtains and a dusting of starlight on the window sill.

It was three o'clock in the morning and the August night was a great bubble of stillness over Colina de Oro. Melinda wiggled gingerly. Her shoulder was enormously sore, but otherwise she felt tickety-boo. She laughed as she caught herself borrowing Robin's word, relieved that she wouldn't have to tell the family about her fall.

She sat up in bed, gazing out of the window, her hands clasped around her knees, thinking about those few moments on the trail when she had returned to consciousness to find Robin carrying her. She felt again his strong, protecting arms around her, his cheek against her hair. He had called her "darling" before he thought. . . . She smiled dreamily at the sickle moon. It looked like a parenthesis at the end of a sentence of stars. Her eyes caressed the familiar, loved hillside, from the shadows of the pepper tree near her window to the fringe of oaks against the skyline. Colina de Oro . . . a horse of her own . . . Robin . . . she held happiness close to her heart.

Somewhere in the night a horse whinnied drowsily. She glanced up at the stables.

And her eyes widened.

Why was the light on in Miguel's room? She could see a chink of brightness under the curtain. Miguel never stayed up until three o'clock in the morning unless something was wrong with one of the horses.

Something wrong with one of the horses...Maybe... *Silverstockings!*

She was out of bed in an instant and slipping into shoes. She forgot all about her sore shoulder as she pulled on her bathrobe. A minute later she went out of the kitchen door and was running up the hill.

She was too intent on her own worry to notice that the barn door was open a little way. Inside, she found the stables in darkness. Feeling her way, she went down the line of stalls. Everything seemed in order. The horses were asleep, Silverstockings a pale gleam in the blackness. She whispered his name and he nuzzled her hand. Ridiculously relieved, she stroked him. But if the horses were all right, why *was* Miguel's light on at three in the morning? Was he ill himself?

She had just felt her way back to the foot of the steep wooden stairway which led up to his quarters when unexpectedly the door at the top opened. There was a moment's shaft of light, then the door closed again and footsteps padded softly down the stairs.

In her astonishment, Melinda slipped to one side and pressed behind a bale of hay, unable to believe her ears.

For there was more than one pair of footsteps.

It was too dark to see. She could only hear the stealthy creak of bare wood, the brush of a hand on the stair rail.

Then, as two dim shapes passed her, she heard the whispered words: "You understand . . . the price of talk?"

"*Sí,*" came Miguel's sullen reply.

Melinda strained for a glimpse of the whisperer. At last, at the stable door, he turned and a ray of starlight fell across his face.

Melinda nearly cried out.

For Miguel's visitor was Chinese—a Chinese whose left eyelid slanted downward in a half-closed droop.

CHAPTER TEN

Enter Jimmy Carter

STUMBLING blindly down the hill, Melinda reached the haven of her room once more without being seen. She shut her window, then sat on the edge of the bed, hands locked in her lap.

It had been frightening enough to hear that chilling whisper in Chinatown in a crowd of people. But now, to know that the same man was coming to Colina de Oro in the middle of the night. . . . She shivered.

Try as she would, she could not escape the fact that all this had only started when Robin entered their lives. A runaway truck, a whispered warning, the man in the mask, an unknown Chinese paying a stealthy visit to their foreman . . .

With her whole heart she wanted to believe that it was all a coincidence. But a small voice at the edge of her mind kept asking: *Is there something Robin is not telling us?*

She tossed until dawn. Then, as another summer day rose on Colina de Oro, she dressed and went up to the stables again.

Miguel was cleaning Silverstockings' stall. Melinda confronted him without warning: "Miguel, who was that Chinese man you were talking to at three o'clock this morning?"

Before she had finished the sentence, the shadowy quiet of the barn was broken by a clatter.

78

Miguel had dropped his broom.

But not before Melinda saw the crafty eyes, quick as a snake's tongue, dart her a strange glance of fear—and defiance.

He picked up the broom. "You dreaming, señorita," he said shortly. "Three o'clock, Miguel in bed. Night come, I sleep. No time for talk."

Melinda interrupted. "I saw him, Miguel. I heard him. I . . . " She stopped, startled at the foreman's twitch of genuine terror. But Miguel did not ask the obvious question: "How did you hear?" Instead, he said with the loudness of panic, "You dreaming. Nobody here last night." Then he turned his back on her in a frenzy of sweeping.

Melinda knew it was useless to ask any more. She gave Silverstockings a kiss, then walked back to the house, frowning to herself.

In the kitchen she found Petunia stirring waffle batter at the big table. Robin was standing on a kitchen chair, with one hand pressed to his heart: "But soft! What light through yonder window breaks? It is the east, and Petunia is the sun!" He finished with an arm sweep that nearly knocked out the light bulb overhead. "Ah, that I were a spoon within that hand!"

Then he climbed down from the chair, remarking modestly, "Shakespeare by Sutherland. An improvement, don't you think?"

Petunia was gazing at him in awe. "Lawzy me, Mr. Robin, you gives me the pin prickles just like Clark Gable."

Melinda burst out laughing.

Robin turned. "Ah, welcome to Stratford on *Oro*, Miss Marshall!" Then his blue eyes sobered and he added softly, "How do you feel?"

"Fine." She smiled. "When you've finished dazzling Petunia, you can help me pick out the jam for breakfast."

In the storeroom, under cover of Petunia singing "Hand Me Down My Bonnet" in her chocolate-fudge voice while she clattered coffee cups, Melinda went on: "Truly, Robin, I feel fine. Oh, a bit sore in spots, and my shoulder is a gorgeous shade of royal purple, but otherwise I'm all right. So keep your promise and don't tell anybody, will you?"

"A Sutherland always keeps his promises," Robin assured her. "And you—you don't know how glad I am that you're tickety-boo!" he added impulsively.

Melinda flashed him a shy smile before turning to the shelves. "Which would you like, blueberry or wild cherry?"

Robin considered his decision long and seriously. "Er . . . what about having a bit of both?"

At breakfast Mrs. Marshall announced that it would be a no-projects day, except that Jimmy Carter was coming to luncheon. Melinda did not miss the note of enthusiasm in her mother's voice. She wondered, smiling to herself, if Jimmy Carter's mother sounded the same way when she learned that he was lunching with the Marshalls.

Robin looked up, interested. But a gentleman doesn't blurt out, "Who's Jimmy Carter?"

He didn't have to. Honey Rose was quick to explain. "Jimmy is Melinda's best beau. He's going to be her partner for the Cotillion."

Melinda stared at her, "Why, Honey Rose, he's just an old friend of the family, and you know it."

Honey Rose did not reply, but her arch sideways smile at Robin conveyed a whole paragraph of "Don't let her fool you. They're practically going steady, so you needn't waste time on Melinda." Then a flutter of eyelashes added, "However, I'm here and very much available."

For the first time in her life Melinda could have cheerfully pushed her pretty cousin into the fishpond.

"I knew a chap from Virginia named Carter," put in Robin tactfully. "He was at Oxford with me. I wonder if they're related."

Five minutes later a dazed Robin had learned that the word "related" is catnip to a Southerner. Honey Rose had given him the genealogy of every Carter family in the South down to whom the second cousins married before Mr. Marshall interrupted with a chuckle, "Wrong number, Honey Rose! Jimmy's father came from Maine."

Honey Rose tossed her silky hair. "*Maine!*" she repeated, as though it were the measles. "You mean they're *Yankees?*"

Mr. Marshall noddd solemnly, but Melinda caught the twinkle in his eyes. "Yes, Honey Rose; and you're on Yankee territory right this minute, don't forget! California abolished slavery before Lincoln did, and we stuck by the Union in the Civil War. Why, before General Sherman marched through Georgia he was manager of a bank in San Francisco!"

Honey Rose gave a delicate pussycat yawn. "I feel just like a nice swim this morning," she changed the subject. "Anybody join me?"

"Aren't you afraid of getting your new bathing suit wet?" asked Melinda sweetly.

Before Honey Rose could answer, Robin turned to Mrs. Marshall. "Looking through my sponge bag this morning I discovered a crisis in razor blades! Would you excuse me for

an hour, Mrs. Marshall, while I run over to Sonoma for some?
Is that the nearest town?"

"Of course, Robin." Mrs. Marshall smiled. "Yes, I think
Sonoma could produce razor blades."

Honey Rose put in quickly: "I've just remembered—I need
some suntan lotion. I'm sure I could get it in Sonoma."

Melinda couldn't resist paying her back for the Jimmy
Carter business. She said innocently, "Oh, you don't have to
bother, Honey Rose. I've got oodles of the sort you use."

Honey Rose shot her a glance that would have wilted a
water lily, but Robin intervened gallantly: "I'd be happy to
get it for you. I won't invite you to go with me, Honey Rose,
as I know you wouldn't want to be seen riding in a—quote
rattletrap sardine can, unquote!"

This time even Honey Rose joined in the laughter.

Melinda waited until Robin had left before speaking to her
father about Miguel and his 3 A.M. visitor. When she finished,
Mr. Marshall's eyes were grave indeed. He did not even take
her to task for investigating a lighted window at that hour of
the night.

"There's something going on. I don't like it."

Pulling the telephone toward him, he dialed a number. A
moment later he was repeating Melinda's story to the sheriff.

When he hung up, Melinda asked, "What did the sheriff
say?"

"Nothing world shaking," her father replied dryly. "They're
going to search the grounds again. Stupid waste of time. What
do they expect—the man to pop out from behind a toyon tree
and introduce himself? They're going to question Miguel,

too." He grinned suddenly. "I must say even the sheriff didn't sound hopeful about that!"

The clock on the mantel struck the hour. "Heavens, it's eleven already," exclaimed Melinda. "I must help Petunia." She blew her father a kiss and slipped out the door.

When she had set the table, shelled the peas, and whipped the cream, there was barely time to change before Jimmy Carter was due. As she brushed her hair, she found herself wondering over and over when Robin would be back. He had been gone way over his hour already.

She heard a car crunch the gravel and ran to the front door.

But it was Jimmy Carter. He waved to her from the driver's seat of a three-tone coupé in shades of chocolate, strawberry, and marshmallow. "Hi, Lindy."

"Hi yourself."

"Made it up from San Francisco in an hour and ten minutes," he announced proudly.

"Fugitive from a soda fountain?" She wrinkled her nose at the car. "Don't you feel awfully conspicuous riding along One-Oh-One in a banana split?"

Jimmy Carter swung a brotherly arm around her shoulder. "Lindy, that buggy's custom painted." His voice was hurt. "Those are the latest colors."

"Latest flavors, you mean," she teased him. "Would you like a swim before lunch?"

They entered the cool dim *corredor* where carnations flared brightly in a silver bowl. "Love it, Lindy, but I've got to be off by three. Being a businessman is heck."

"Poor Jimmy, you're just fading away," grinned Melinda, surveying his husky, broad-shouldered frame. There was so *much* of Jimmy Carter. His parents had been too conscientious with the cod-liver oil and orange juice when he was a baby. He wasn't as tall as Robin but what there was took up lots more room, especially with Jimmy's habit of draping his arms like a weary windmill over the nearest object. He had a shock of tousled brown hair, hazel eyes that were kind and honest behind the horn-rimmed glasses he wore under the happy delusion that they made him look older and wiser, a generous mouth, ears that would have made Dumbo jealous, and a very high opinion of his own brilliance. His father owned a big machinery company in San Francisco, and Jimmy was starting in at what he called the bottom for a month before being made vice president—he hoped.

"Sorry I couldn't get up here yesterday. But I didn't forget you." From a pocket of his black-and-white striped sports coat which looked to Melinda like a pedestrian crossing, he extracted a long box and handed it to her. "Just a little memento ahead of time of our big date."

"Jimmy, how sweet of you." Quickly she tore off paper and ribbon. "My Cotillion gloves. You *are* a dear!"

Jimmy was turning pink around the ears, which meant, with Jimmy, that there was quite a lot of pink. He shifted from one foot to the other, always a sign that he wanted to say something but didn't know how. Melinda waited patiently until he finally blurted out: "Well, I didn't really think of it myself. I never know what to give a girl, so I asked Mom. She suggested them."

Melinda lifted out the long regulation sixteen-button white-kid gloves. "I don't care whose idea they were, they're from *you*, Jimmy. You're the one I'll think of when I'm wearing them, and you're the one I'm thanking, heaps and heaps!"

She gave him a quick tiptoe kiss on the cheek, then held out her hand. "Come on, let's find the family."

She said "family," but her eyes strayed to the front door. Could Robin have gotten lost? The Valley of the Moon was full of winding back roads.

Luncheon had been planned for twelve-thirty, but as there was nothing that would spoil, Mrs. Marshall suggested that they wait another half-hour.

"Fine," agreed Jimmy. "How about showing me some of the birthday loot, Lindy?"

"Oh, you're going to be introduced to my gorgeousest present after lunch," Melinda promised him. "But meanwhile I'll show you the beautiful cross Doña Ysabel gave me, and my horseshoe cuff links. . . ."

"Cuff links? Better keep 'em in the safe while I'm around!"

Melinda laughed and went down the hall to her room. On the way she passed Robin's door. It was open, and she glanced in as she went by to see whether Petunia had closed the curtains against the hot afternoon sun.

She sighed with envy at Robin's neatness. If only her room looked like this—just once in a while! There were only a pair of good brushes, a long-handled bone shoehorn, and an electric razor on the bureau; and a framed photograph on the desk of an attractive older woman in evening dress with a feathery diamond tiara. Robin looked like her, thought Melinda.

And then suddenly, as she pulled the blinds, the significance of one of those items arranged with such British officer's precision on the bureau leaped out at her.

The electric razor!

So it *wasn't* razor blades that Robin had gone to Sonoma for, after all.

CHAPTER ELEVEN

Departure

PUZZLED, Melinda went into her room. What *was* Robin doing in Sonoma that took so long and why did he have to make up a reason for it?

Then, as she returned to the patio with her gifts to show Jimmy, the telephone rang.

A moment later Mr. Marshall came out. "That was Robin Sutherland," he told them. "He's very sorry but he must miss lunch. Lightnin' Bug came down with the wheezles just as they reached Sonoma."

Even Jimmy, who was seldom aware of anything unless it hit him in the solar plexus, noticed Melinda's disappointment.

"Robin Sutherland. Isn't that the hero of the runaway truck?"

Melinda straightened with pride. "I wanted you to meet him. I know you'd like him."

"If he's a friend of yours ... well, I'd do my best!" he answered gamely. "By the way, Lindy," he added as they sat down to luncheon in the patio, "any news yet from Stanford?"

"You mean my application? Not yet. But I'm still hoping."

Honey Rose was helping Petunia serve creamed chicken and spoon bread. "Was Stanford named for a person, like

Duke University or William and Mary?" she asked. "Or was the town called Stanford first?"

It was Doña Ysabel who answered, her hair smoky silver in the sun. "No, Stanford is in the town of Palo Alto. It was named for a person—a fifteen-year-old boy who died of fever in Italy nearly a hundred years ago. His name was Leland Stanford, Junior, and that's really the university's correct title."

"You mean it's Leland Stanford Junior University?" asked Melinda in surprise. "Nobody ever calls it that. Who was he?"

"The dearly loved son of one of the men who built the Central Pacific Railroad in the sixties. His father was wealthy, powerful, a governor of California, one of the towering figures of the West. As the Spanish say: he lifted the rainbow on his shoulders! And he had a dream: that California should one day have a university which would equal the great colleges of the East. After his son's death on a trip to Florence, he and his wife said, 'The children of California shall be our children.' So they went back to Harvard to see President Charles W. Eliot and ask him how one starts a university."

"That was a tall order." Jimmy grinned, hoping that no one was noticing his third helping of spoon bread. "I'll bet Eliot was surprised."

"Indeed he was. Unfortunately he was also very condescending to this simply dressed stranger and his wife who didn't look as though they could afford a carriage of their own. And when Mr. Stanford came straight to the point and asked, 'How much would it cost to duplicate Harvard?' President Eliot gasped. He thought they were joking. He decided to name a ridiculously huge sum which would end this meeting at once. 'About twenty-five million dollars,' he answered curtly. Leland Stanford turned to his wife"—Doña Ysabel's jewel-freighted hands flew wide—" 'Jane, we can do it!' he cried, 'we can do it!' ''

Mrs. Marshall smiled. "Really, Ysabel, you should have been an actress!"

Even Petunia had stopped in the doorway with a tray of pecan pie to listen, wide-eyed.

"And they did do it," concluded Doña Ysabel. "Leland Stanford Junior University opened in 1891, one of the great colleges of the world—a memorial to an only son."

"Gosh," murmured Jimmy reverently.

After luncheon Melinda took Jimmy up the hill to introduce him to Silverstockings. As they were coming out of the stables, Jimmy glanced at his watch. "Heck, it's half-past two already. Got to get back to the grind. I've said good-by to your parents." He touched her hand awkwardly. "Don't forget me, will you, Lindy?"

She walked around to the front driveway with him. "Come again soon, Jimmy," she said, and tried to sound as though she meant it.

He closed her fingers in his cannonball of a fist for a final crushing good-by, and then the car was roaring up the drive in a cloud of dust. At the top of the hill he turned and waved.

Melinda waved back and then went into the house.

In the *corredor* she met her father. "The sheriff just phoned," he told her. "He searched the grounds again and questioned Miguel. As we expected, he drew a blank."

"Wh—what do we do next?"

"Not much we can do, except keep our eyes open and take

no chances." Then, seeing her anxious look, he gently lifted her chin with his forefinger. "And keep smiling, Baby!"

But after he went back to his study, Melinda still felt restless and uneasy. On an impulse she slipped along the hall to Doña Ysabel's room. The Spanish dowager always took a siesta in the afternoon, resting on the sofa in an antique brocade dressing gown.

Melinda knocked softly. "Are you asleep, Doña Ysabel?"

"Certainly not," was the brisk response. "Come in, child. I may be old but I'm not that old!"

Melinda went in and settled herself on the footstool beside the sofa. "You're *not* old," she protested fiercely. "Not the least little bit."

Her godmother smiled. "I don't mind, my dear. It isn't how many pages there are in your book of years that matter, but what you write on them. If every chapter is bright with love and laughter, with the crimson of courage and the gold of giving, then when you have written the last page you can read it over and be content."

"What a wonderful book *you* have to read over," whispered Melinda.

Doña Ysabel turned her head away. "Some of my pages were blotted with tears, child. I pray that the Holy Angels will spare you those."

Melinda knew that her godmother was thinking of the young Englishman who had died out in India. She said nothing, but laid her head for a moment on her godmother's hand, feeling its coolness like old satin against her cheek.

"Melinda," asked Doña Ysabel after a pause, "you are in love with Robin Sutherland?"

The casualness of the question took Melinda's breath away.

You couldn't be in love with someone you'd known only a week.

Or could you?

She avoided Doña Ysabel's searching eyes. "I ... I don't know."

"Hmmm," said Doña Ysabel. After a minute she went on, almost as though she were talking to herself. "Robin Sutherland is a gentleman. By that I mean a man so strong and fearless that he can be truly gentle. He has courtesy. He has humor. He has integrity. He also has a brain. His is not a mind like a juke box which loudly plays the current popular opinion. He thinks for himself. All this I believe. But I do not for a moment believe that such a man is here in America merely to write articles. He has come for something else." She crossed her thin hands in her lap and looked straight at Melinda. "Has he told you what it is?"

Melinda shook her head. "No. But I've thought of that, too."

Doña Ysabel smoothed a fold of black brocade. Her Spanish profile was pale and fine-boned as a cameo against the ruby velvet curtains behind her. "He will tell you, my child. In his own time he will tell you. When he has proved you worthy of his confidence."

"I ... I hope so," whispered Melinda. She was on the point of confiding to her godmother some of the disturbing events of the past few days and asking her advice, when suddenly there was a roar that sounded like an express train coming up the driveway.

Doña Ysabel burst into laughter. "As the Super Chief does not run through Colina de Oro, that must be the señor we speak of. Run along and meet him, dear."

Melinda needed no urging. At the door she stopped long enough to blow her godmother a quick over-the-shoulder kiss.

"And for heaven's sake, child, don't let Honey Rose walk off with him," added Doña Ysabel.

Melinda stared at her, then giggled and sped off down the hall. Not much escaped Doña Ysabel!

She reached the front door just as Robin pushed it open from the other side. "I say, Melinda, I'm awfully sorry to have been gone so long." He greeted her warmly. "Lightnin' Bug broke down and I had to take it to the doctor. I spent most of the time convincing the garage that I did *not* need a de-icer, a built-in barbecue, or a horn which plays 'Rule Britannia,' and that four new tires would be a grave shock to Lightnin' Bug's system after a lifetime diet of one secondhand retread every two years."

He was talking with his usual wry gaiety, but he looked hot and dusty and—discouraged, thought Melinda in surprise.

"Speaking of diet, how about a nice tall glass of iced coffee right now and a piece of Petunia's pecan pie?"

With feminine instinct, Melinda had lighted unerringly upon the one guaranteed perker-upper for discouraged gentlemen.

"Do you really mean it? How glorious! I'll be there in a second, as soon as I wash off a layer or two of Sonoma County."

Melinda had just made a fresh glass of iced coffee when Robin joined her in the kitchen.

"*Oh, never say that I was false of heart,*" he greeted Petunia with clasped hands, "*though absence seemed my flame to qualify* . . . I could smell that pie in Sonoma!"

Petunia gazed at him in rapture.

Robin picked up the tray. "No wonder they named California for a corner of heaven," he remarked, looking at the full quarter of pie that Petunia had saved for him.

But once with Robin in a shady corner of the patio, while he made short work of coffee and pie, Melinda could not bring herself to ask him about the razor blades or the real reason he had been gone so long that morning. It was enough that he was home again—and safely.

The week flew by in a round of rides, swims, and picnics, and there were no more mysterious or frightening events.

The time passed so quickly that Melinda could hardly believe it when the day came for Robin to leave.

"We're sorry to have you go, Robin," said Mrs. Marshall at breakfast the last morning.

"I shall certainly hope to see you all again before I go home."

The words "go home" sent a surprising little stab through Melinda's heart. Home was so far away.

"Of course we'll see you again," stated his hostess. "In fact, will you be around during the middle of September? Would you like to come to the opening of the opera with us? That's a San Francisco tradition you should add to your collection."

Melinda drew a quick breath. One of the big events of the year, and here Mums was inviting Robin as casually as though their box held sixteen chairs instead of six. Dearly as she had always loved her mother, she especially adored her at that moment.

Robin's face lighted. "There's nothing I'd like more. Thanks awfully, Mrs. Marshall."

"Then you'd better stay with us that night. Oh, it's formal, I'm afraid." She hesitated, wondering if a young Englishman exploring America in an MG would have white tie and tails with him.

"Naturally."

There was something in the way Robin said it that reminded Melinda of stories she'd read about Englishmen sitting down to solitary jungle chicken in a tropical bungalow or dining alone in the Australian bush, always in a dinner jacket. Up to now she'd thought it rather silly. But suddenly in that one word of Robin's she caught a glimpse of the reason behind it. Changing for dinner in a far-flung outpost wasn't being stuffy or affected. It just meant that you were taking with you to the frontiers of the world the small niceties of life which had made you what you were.

After breakfast the whole family helped Robin load his gear into Lightnin' Bug, then gathered to wave good-by. Robin's tanned face was flushed with gratitude as he thanked each of them in turn for "such a w-w-wonderful week."

But when he reached Doña Ysabel, a strange thing happened.

A trick of the sunlight made her thin face transparent for an instant, and he caught a glimpse of the stirringly beautiful young girl she must have been . . . so long ago. Involuntarily he gave her the frankly admiring smile that a man gives a lovely girl.

Startled, she looked into his eyes. Then, with an effort as though it were a long and unwilling journey, she stepped back into the shadow of the doorway. Once again she became only a very old lady in black velvet and creamy lace. "*Vaya con Dios*, Robin Sutherland." She smiled wistfully. "Go with God."

Out in the driveway, as Robin folded himself up into

Lightnin' Bug, he turned to Melinda. "Like a ride to the top of the hill?" he asked impulsively.

The answer was obvious.

At the crest Robin pulled up, then sat for a moment looking down on the hollow in the hills. "I'll miss Colina de Oro," he said softly, "the red tiles and the pepper tree, and the shape of the shadows under the eaves." He paused and looked at her. "And I shall miss the people who live there."

Melinda's heart skipped a beat. He was looking at her with an expression that was no help at all for a poised reply. "I . . . we'll miss you, too, Robin," she managed at last. "And . . . Oh, Robin, do take care of yourself!"

He reached over and took both her hands in his. "Don't worry, I'll be all right."

And then, before she knew what he was going to do, Robin had raised her hand and held it against his cheek for an instant.

Something in the quick, boyish gesture sent a greater thrill through Melinda than if he had kissed her good-by. Never would she forget the shy tenderness of that touch.

Then she got out of the car and he drove away.

A streak of yellow curving out of sight along the bumpy road . . . and she was left alone with only a shaft of golden sunlight between the toyon trees to mark the way he had gone.

CHAPTER TWELVE

Spun Sugar and Angels' Wings

THE ranch seemed very empty after Robin left. Melinda was more grateful than ever for Silverstockings' company.

A thank-you letter from Robin duly arrived for Mrs. Marshall; but after that, with the exception of a polite post card to Honey Rose, Robin's letters all bore the address *Miss Melinda Marshall.*

They were long, wonderful, funny letters, and she read them over and over. He did not stay long in Carmel but went on to Los Angeles where he reported changing Lightnin' Bug's name to Old Faithful because the radiator boiled over regularly every hour in the Southern California heat. After that he returned to Santa Barbara and devoted one whole letter to telling Melinda all about the California missions: how the chain was started in 1769 at San Diego by the Majorca-born Franciscan monk, Fra Junípero Serra (who named San Francisco for the Founder of his Order, Saint Francis of Assisi), how they were spaced a day's walk apart up the coast, and how they brought education and health and Christianity to the Indians, not to mention the first dates (palms were planted at each mission to supply fronds for Good Friday), and the first California oranges.

None of which was exactly news to a girl whose ancestors had accompanied Father Serra on his journey.

And then, incredibly, the summer was over and it was time for the Marshall family to say good-by to Doña Ysabel and move back to San Francisco, bringing Silverstockings down to a stable in Marin County.

As soon as they were in town once more, Melinda and her mother started hunting for her ball gown for the Cotillion. This was no spur-of-the-minute choice. Next to her wedding gown, it would probably be the most important dress she would ever have. Mrs. Marshall wanted something long and white and easy to curtsy in. Melinda merely wanted the most beautiful dress in the whole world.

But at last, after days of searchings and tryings-on and not-quite's, they found it.

It was love at first fitting. Creamy parchment brocade, demure bodice, a sweep of skirt caught up with clusters of white violets.

Melinda circled in it slowly before the dressing-room mirror, her amber eyes glowing. "Oh, Mums, isn't it *glor-geous?*"

Mums was a little startled. She had never thought of her frisky colt of a daughter as beautiful before. But in this dress, with her golden hair and the little enamel cross and long white gloves.... "Yes, Baby, it's just *glor-geous,*" she agreed. Turning to the saleswoman, she asked the price.

The saleswoman told her.

"Ohhhh," said Melinda, and it sounded like the little sigh when you let the air out of a balloon.

"It's an exclusive, you see, madam."

"Very," agreed Mrs. Marshall with feeling. She turned to

Melinda. "We're lunching with Daddy at the Ritz Old Poodle Dog. We'll see what he says." But she gave Melinda the ghost of a wink.

The Ritz Old Poodle Dog was one of the oldest restaurants in San Francisco, and close to the Montgomery Street district where Mr. Marshall had his office.

Now a canyon of steel and concrete, the "Wall Street of the West," Melinda found it hard to believe that a little more than a hundred years ago Montgomery Street had been the shore line—a shore line bordered by a sandy waste called El Parage de Yerba Buena, The Place of the Good Herb, from the aromatic mint that grew there. (But no flowers bloomed among the sand dunes in those days. One San Francisco beau scoured the town for a bouquet for his girl and finally paid five dollars—for five geranium leaves!)

However, Montgomery Street is far from being the shore line today. When the Gold Rush brought thousands swarming to the gold fields, California's population jumped from fifteen thousand to more than six hundred thousand in two years. The result, strangely enough, was to turn San Francisco temporarily into a ghost town. Everyone left his job and home to join in the feverish digging in the Mother Lode country. Food soared in price, postage jumped to four dollars a letter, shops were closed.

And no sooner did a ship drop anchor along Montgomery Street than the sailors deserted to join the Gold Rush. Eventually there were more than five hundred tall, proud, empty sailing ships tied up along the shore; a lonely forest of masts and rigging that creaked eerily in the fog and echoed to the meeows of ships' cats prowling in the moonlight.

But as San Francisco gradually returned to normal, there

was a desperate need for more houses and shops and buildings for all those who decided to stay and make their homes in the new land. So the deserted ships were pressed into service as hotels and offices, linked by footbridges.

Then slowly the water between them became filled in, too; and at last even the ships themselves were absorbed into the made land, until today skyscrapers rise above their skeletons.

As Melinda and her mother walked toward the Ritz Old Poodle Dog, they suddenly heard a voice behind them: "Well, don't tell me that you were actually going to be *on time* for once!"

They turned to see Mr. Marshall emerging from a tall office building. He greeted his wife with a kiss and grinned at Melinda. "Any luck with the dress today?"

Mother and daughter exchanged conspirators' glances.

"We'll tell you all about that at luncheon, dear," said his wife quickly; "you must be hungry."

"Goodness, is it *that* expensive?" groaned Mr. Marshall.

Slowly they edged their way through the noon-hour crowds of businessmen in dark suits and white shirts and secretaries in dark skirts and white blouses, the Montgomery Street "uniform."

"Not like the good old days, is it?" remarked Mr. Marshall.

As the "good old days" with Daddy could mean anything from the early Christian martyrs to the week before they bought a television set, Melinda asked, "Which ones?"

"Around 1870."

"That must have been before you married me, darling," murmured Mrs. Marshall sweetly.

Her husband chuckled. "The women had long, swishy silk dresses then, with bonnets and black lace shawls; and the men wore Prince Albert coats, pale golden-brown vests, yellow gloves, big white sombreros . . ."

"They must have looked like lemon meringue pie," put in his wife.

". . . and you could always tell a man's profession from his jewelry. A gambler had diamond shirt buttons and diamond cuff links; a miner had a gold watch that weighed one pound, no more, no less. Then there were the Mexicans in their red sashes and striped serapes, and the Spanish girls wearing thickly pleated cotton print skirts. And always, padding through the crowd in their blue blouses with queues hanging from the back of their heads, the Chinese who had been brought over to work on the railroad."

"Who's working on the railroad?" a familiar but puzzled voice suddenly broke in from somewhere above Melinda's head.

She turned quickly, to see Jimmy Carter's football shoulders towering over her. "Why, hello there, Jimmy."

Mrs. Marshall, as usual, made no secret of her pleasure at encountering Jimmy; and somehow, before Melinda was quite aware of it, Jimmy had been invited to join them for luncheon.

He fell into step beside Melinda and took her arm in a proprietary grip. "This'll pep me up. Honest, Lindy, there's nothing like hard work to wear you out."

"Especially when you're not used to it," murmured Melinda wickedly.

"Where's Honey Rose?" he asked, tweaking her little finger.

"Having her eighty-ninth manicure or something. My, I'm hungry," she added as they entered the restaurant and were shown to Mr. Marshall's regular table.

As soon as they were seated, Mr. Marshall looked around the group. "Correct me if I'm wrong, everybody, but you, my dear, want one small lamb chop and, for a special treat, a stalk of celery, while Melinda and Jimmy are probably dying of starvation. Lucky I have only one daughter to feed; otherwise I'd go into *bankrupture* as Petunia calls it."

"But you know, sir," suggested Jimmy after they'd ordered, "back in the days when people had big families things didn't cost as much; it sort of evens up. I mean, well, look at this luncheon."

"I am," his host assured him, "and faced with your appetite and Melinda's I find the prospect alarming."

Jimmy grinned. "What I mean is, just sixty or seventy years ago, why, it wouldn't have cost nearly this much."

Mr. Marshall sighed theatrically. "You could get a decent meal for twenty cents, and for fifty you could have a banquet. But the funny thing is that just a few years before that, back in the fifties and sixties, coins below a quarter were a great rarity in California. If a bill came out unevenly, the clerk always knocked off any odd amount up to twenty-five cents."

"How nice," exclaimed Mrs. Marshall. "Why?"

"Because they just didn't have any dimes, nickels, and pennies out in the West yet. Eventually that habit of knocking off the odd pennies gave a word to our language. Most people think of it as slang, but it isn't. It came from the constant phrase in the California of the sixties: 'Never mind the bits, madam.' Gradually a *bit* came to have a definite value, one eighth of a dollar, or half of the lowest silver coin they had in circulation then. What's the matter, Melinda, are you going into a trance?"

Melinda was sitting with her eyes closed while her lips

moved soundlessly. At her father's question she giggled. "I'm working out how much my Cotillion dress would cost in 'bits.' "

"Oh, have you found it?" asked Jimmy. "What's it like?"

Melinda glanced at her mother. "It's—it's moonlight and stardust and spun sugar and angels' wings!"

Jimmy's eyes grew round behind his terribly-intellectual spectacles. "That," he said, "will be something to see."

"And just how much," inquired Mr. Marshall, "are angels' wings this year?"

"They're not cheap, dear," murmured his wife. "They have to be imported, you know."

Her husband grinned, then looked across at Melinda. "Sure it's the right one, Baby?" he asked softly.

Crossing her fingers under the table, Melinda nodded. Then she waited.

"If that's the case," harrumphed her father with the gruffness which meant that he was being softhearted and hoped nobody noticed, "I can see where I'm going into *bankrupture*, after all."

"Oh, Daddy!" Heedless of onlookers at other tables, Melinda jumped up and threw her arms rapturously around his neck. "Oh, Daddy, you *angel!*"

"Naturally," agreed Mr. Marshall, "where else were you planning to get those wings?"

CHAPTER THIRTEEN

Unexpected Visitor

THE opening of the opera was the following day.

Shortly after luncheon the telephone rang. At the first "Good afternoon, my dear Miss Marshall," Melinda's heart took off on a rocket.

"Robin! Where are you?"

"At Much-Pottering-Under-Oaks . . . on the way to San Francisco and you."

"Where?" Melinda stared at the receiver.

"That's what we'd call it at home. You probably just call it Burlingame—very dull! How are you?"

"Tickety-boo!"

Robin's chuckle came over the wire. "Same here. And I can't wait for tonight. I say, Melinda, could I come a bit early and change at your house? Lightnin' Bug's rather a tight fit for a dressing room."

"Come right away," replied Melinda eagerly. "We all have to be at the Museum of Art for early supper anyway; Mums is a hostess."

"Thanks awfully. I'll be there in an hour. And . . . . Oh, bother, any second now a polite voice is going to ask me for more money for this trunk call. And it's not going to be impressed when I offer it a nice, shiny sixpence. I'll finish when I see you. Cheerio, Melinda."

"Cheerio, Robin!" Hanging up, she floated back to her room on a rose-tinted cloud.

By dint of putting vitamin pills in the petrol, or so he said, Robin arrived at Pacific Heights in just fifty minutes and came bounding up the steps.

"Melinda!" He smothered her outstretched hand in both of his.

"Hello Robin Petunia fixed some tea for you I thought you might be hungry," she greeted him all in one breath.

"You're ministering angels, both of you! I say, Melinda," he added softly, "it's awfully g-g-good to see you again."

"It's . . . it's good to see you, Robin." She wondered why her heart was behaving like a runaway cable car as they went out to the kitchen. Maybe it was because Robin had forgotten to let go of her hand.

"How's Doña Ysabel?" he wanted to know.

"Wonderful as ever, and she's really looking forward to coming down here for my debut at Christmas. Although it will be the first time she's left the ranch since . . . oh, since before I was born. How do you like your tea?" Melinda uncovered a plate of deviled-crab sandwiches.

"Milk and sugar and strong enough to float Her Majesty's Navy, please!"

After making a thorough job of the crab sandwiches, and halfway through his third slice of coconut cake, Robin suddenly glanced at his watch. "By Jove, it's four-thirty! Doesn't a girl usually take hours to dress for a big evening?"

Melinda shook her head. "Not me. I'll be waiting downstairs before you are!"

Robin rose from the table. "We'll see about that, young lady!"

The dressing race ended in a draw, for instead of meeting at the foot of the stairs, they met in the upstairs hall.

Robin looked older in his white tie and tails, and very handsome. Melinda felt suddenly shy, like a little girl, in her blue velvet with the heirloom lace collar.

Robin surveyed her from the velvet slippers to her brushed-to-a-gleam hair, and he didn't miss the little gold lion on the chain around her wrist. "How perfectly lovely you look."

His tone sent her confidence soaring. "I thought this dress was awfully young," she confided, her fingers resting shyly on his arm as they went downstairs together.

"What do you want to be—*elderly?*" demanded Robin. "You know, Melinda, you're not the sequins-and-spike-heels type, thank heaven. You never will be even when you're a hundred. Anybody can be sophisticated if they haven't got anything else. You have. Something rather special. You're the . . . the puffed-sleeves and wild r-r-roses and a single-strand-of-real-pearls type."

Melinda blushed happily.

And changed her mind about telling Robin the Sad Saga of the Earrings.

She had started out for the evening in a pair of six-inch rhinestone chandeliers that tickled her neck deliciously, when Honey Rose, with a "Horrors, my pet!" had highhandedly removed them. Of course the earrings *were* Honey Rose's, but at the time she had thought it most uncousinly. Now she was just the tiniest bit glad.

Mrs. Marshall joined them in the living room. "It's so nice to see you again," she welcomed Robin with a warm smile. Then she turned to Melinda. "Baby, I can't find my new evening gloves anywhere."

"You put them in the Enchanted Forest, Mums, don't you remember?"

"Oh, dear," sighed Mrs. Marshall. And her opera gown of pink peonies on silver damask sighed faintly, too, as she sank onto the sofa. "That's so far away."

Robin jumped up, reminding Melinda of a gallant knight springing to the rescue of a lady in distress. "May I fetch them for you, Mrs. Marshall? Which is the path to the Enchanted Forest?"

Mother and daughter laughed together. "It's our attic," Melinda explained. "We call it that because when you go up there to look for something, it's so hard to find your way out again! I'll run up for them. Anything else, Mums?"

"You might bring my opera glasses. I *think* they're in that big box under the pile of *Geographics* marked 'Melinda's Christening Robe.' "

Melinda was gone several minutes. She found the gloves right away, but the opera glasses took real detective work. As she returned, a drift of languorous perfume told her that Honey Rose had already gone down; and she heard the voice of the Baron de Palafox in the living room.

After greeting the baron, Melinda gave the gloves and the glasses to her mother. "They weren't in the christening-robe box, Mums. They were in the bottom of the chest with Daddy's jodhpur boots and your riding crop."

"They *were?* Oh, yes, I remember. I thought I'd want them for the horse show and if I put them in with our riding things, then I wouldn't forget where I'd put them, and . . . ."

"Do you and your husband ride in horse shows?" asked Robin with interest.

"Oh, dear, no," replied Mrs. Marshall, "we just go to them." She rose from the sofa with an angelic smile. "We really ought to be leaving. Where is that husband of mine?"

"Here, darling." Mr. Marshall appeared in the doorway and bowed to them all. "Mrs. Charles Marshall wore an original in pink-and-silver brocade," he quoted the society editors, "Mr. Marshall wore pencil-slim black with touches of white at throat and wrist, the latest mode in pearl cuff links, and a tastefully tied white tie which is giving him apoplexy. Good evening, everybody."

The flurry of laughter that greeted him was followed by another flurry of looking for Mrs. Marshall's evening bag, and then the baron turned to Honey Rose. "Will you do me the honor of coming with me, mademoiselle? Melinda can show Monsieur Rob-een the way in his car."

Honey Rose, all glitter and glamour and dangling the white-fox cape referred to ungallantly by Mr. Marshall as "Honey's Bowwows," didn't look as though this was quite the arrangement she had hoped for. But she accepted politely, and waited while the baron negotiated the steps on his crutches.

Twenty minutes later, when Melinda and Robin arrived at the Museum of Art next door to the Opera House where the annual opening-night supper is held, they were cordially greeted by Mrs. Marshall who said how delighted she was to see them, and how good it was of them to come.

Robin looked so stunned that Melinda had to whisper to

him, "Mums always gets that glazed look at big functions where she has to greet hundreds of people."

"But doesn't she realize it's *us?*"

"Probably not," replied Melinda serenely. "Oh, hello there, Jimmy."

Jimmy Carter was shouldering his way through the crowd like a cheerful bull moose in glasses. "Hi, Lindy."

After Melinda introduced him, Robin found his hand crushed in an overwhelming grip. "I've heard a lot about you. Glad to meet you."

"I'm happy to meet you." Robin retrieved his hand gingerly.

There was a pause. The two men's happiness to meet each other did not seem to extend to further conversation, so Melinda broke the silence by announcing, "I never thought I'd be hungry, but I am."

"So am I!" Jimmy's face lighted up at this discovery of a kindred soul. "Let's get started."

The buffet was good, catered by an exotic South Seas restaurant; and the decorations of red roses and frilly fans took their cue from the evening's opera, *La Traviata.*

Ample time before the first curtain the warning signal was given. As they went out, Mrs. Marshall was standing near the door. "Oh, there you are. Now if only Charles were here."

"Charles *is,*" said a patient voice behind her, "only nobody notices, as usual."

"Why, darling, as if they could help it, you look so handsome tonight." With a disarming, wifely smile, Mrs. Marshall took his arm to lead the way.

As they crossed the open parkway toward the majestic War Memorial Opera House, twilight folded gauzy wings over the tall gold-and-black iron gates, and muted the columned stone façade into a velvety blur. Automobile lights paved Van Ness Avenue with a bracelet of rubies and diamonds; while across the street in its halo of spotlights the great soaring dome of City Hall, copied after the Capitol in Washington, hung like a frosted bell from the lacquer-blue sky.

There was a tingle of expectancy in the air. Even the crowds watching the audience arrive had the keyed-up air of a family party. It didn't matter whether they could afford seats or not, whether they would see the golden curtain rise or only stand outside and earnestly discuss Verdi, this evening belonged to everybody in San Francisco. It was their own special opera, and they were intensely, personally proud of it.

The Marshall party went in through the carriage entrance, past a cluster of photographers. Their popping flash bulbs left whizzing red suns inside Melinda's eyelids when she shut her eyes.

The central foyer was packed. The kaleidoscope of dresses, jewels, furs, color, perfume, and chatter left Melinda blinking and dizzy, and more than ever conscious of her plain blue velvet. Maybe the collar was a treasured heirloom, but who would even notice it in that jewel-encrusted swirl?

Suddenly she found Robin's hand under her arm, guiding her across the marble floor. "You look just like a real blossom which has strayed into a shop of artificial flowers," he murmured.

It was as though someone had lighted a candle near her heart.

When the bell rang for the last time, they went up to the Marshall box. Although she had been to the Opera House many times, Melinda never got over that first little quickening thrill as she came into the great, softly lighted auditorium with its tremendous chandelier of Philippine shell, a sunburst of lavender and gold in the center of the ceiling; and its bigger-than-life gold horses galloping across the proscenium arch above the stage.

"But I'd take Silverstockings any day," Robin whispered in Melinda's ear.

She smiled at him, then drew a happy breath as the orchestra began tuning up like a chorus of excited crickets. A few minutes later, settling back in her small gold chair, she gave herself up to the gay and poignant beauty of *La Traviata*.

During the intermission Mr. and Mrs. Marshall and Honey Rose strolled in the foyer greeting friends, but Melinda and Robin stayed with the crippled baron, who wanted to hear all about Robin's recent travels throughout California.

When the opera was over and the principals had taken their last curtain call and Melinda had unwillingly returned to the everyday twentieth century, they went out to their cars. Mr. and Mrs. Marshall, Honey Rose and the baron had all been invited to one of the many after-the-opera supper parties on Nob Hill; but Melinda had not yet "come out," so she and Robin headed for Lightnin' Bug and home.

It was almost midnight as they drove back to Pacific Heights. The stars were a black-and-white reflection of the technicolor galaxy of the city spread out below them; while the dark waters of the Bay repeated in splintered topaz the chain of yellow lights outlining the Golden Gate Bridge.

As they went up the steps of the house, Melinda noticed that Petunia had left the light on in the living room. Fishing in her bag for the door key, she handed it to Robin.

In the hall, Robin shut the door softly behind him. "Should we tell Petunia we're home?"

Melinda did not answer for a second. She was suddenly conscious of a wisp of familiar fragrance. Light, sweet, it tugged at her memory. Mums didn't wear that perfume. Certainly it wasn't one of Honey Rose's *Amour* Something or Other.

"Robin, do you smell *perfume?*"

Robin stopped. "You're right. Now where have I smelled that recently? It's . . . it's like damask roses."

"Damask roses?" Melinda stared at him. "*It can't be.*"

Even as she spoke, a voice came to them through the open door of the living room. Soft, low, vibrant as a plucked harp string.

"Melinda, Robin, come here. I must speak with you."

Melinda spun around. Then she and Robin hurried to the living-room door.

An erect black-clad figure sat enthroned in a small blue-satin chair in front of the drawn curtains.

Robin bowed. "*Buenas noches*, Doña Ysabel." He smiled.

CHAPTER FOURTEEN

Robin's Story

D OÑA YSABEL," gasped Melinda, "what's happened?"
The Spanish dowager merely motioned them to the
sofa. "How much time have we?"

Melinda glanced at the clock. "It will be at least two hours
before the others get home."

"Good." Doña Ysabel paused. Then: "At three o'clock
this morning I awoke to find a man looking in my bedroom
window."

Melinda's heart turned over.

Robin leaned forward. "A *prowler?*" His voice was suddenly tense. "What did you do?"

"As he crept around the corner of the house, I said, 'My
friend, what is it that you seek?' " Doña Ysabel smiled wryly.
"He disappeared into the shadows like quicksilver in sand.
In the morning I sent for the sheriff. When I described him,
the sheriff surprised me greatly. He said that you had already
seen the man before."

"Not a Chinese," whispered Melinda, "with a drooping
eyelid?"

Her godmother nodded.

"*Chinese?*" repeated Robin in amazement.

Quickly Melinda related where she had seen him before.

When she finished, Robin turned to Doña Ysabel. "But why do you come to *us* about it, señora?"

Doña Ysabel paused before she answered. Then she said, "You did not come to America only to write articles and see the country, did you, my son?"

There was a long silence.

"How did you know that, Doña Ysabel?" asked Robin at last.

"Strange and sinister events do not follow in the footsteps of an ordinary tourist."

"But they can't have anything to do with *me*." Robin was frowning. "Because I didn't tell anybody the real reason I came over. I mean ... it's so personal and it sounds rather mad. And yet, it's terribly important."

"Tell us, my son," commanded Doña Ysabel.

Robin sat back. "I believe I'd better. I've been longing to talk it over with someone, get a new perspective." He turned to Melinda. "You don't know how often I've nearly told you. But it's a long story. Actually it starts back in 1840. As you know, Doña Ysabel, in the early days California was a Mexican province. But the Californianos were always revolting, and the authorities lived in perpetual jitters. The foreigners didn't help either, Americans, Europeans, Englishmen, most of whom entered the country ... er ... informally." He grinned. "My own great-great-grandfather jumped ship in San Francisco. But he wasn't one of the troublemakers. He settled down on a farm and sent for his wife, Arabella, from England. Arabella brought their few treasures, a cradle, books, her paints—she was a very good miniature artist. Farm life was hard work, but they were happy together, and my great-grandfather, Carlton, was born there in the wilderness."

"Where was their farm?" asked Doña Ysabel.

"If I knew that, señora, I wouldn't be here," answered Robin simply. "Arabella's letters home to her father never mentioned nearby towns. Probably there weren't any. Their mail was sent care of a friend in San Francisco who later disappeared."

Robin drew a deep breath. "Arabella and her husband would probably have lived out their lives in peace and obscurity if, in the distant town of Natividad, an American fur trapper named Isaac Graham hadn't begun brewing home-distilled *aguardiente* . . . ."

"Wheat whisky, more vicious than a timber wolf," explained Doña Ysabel to Melinda.

"Most of the fur trappers were honest, courageous men—they blazed the overland trails later followed by the covered wagons—but Graham was the ringleader of all the lawbreaking, troublemaking foreigners in California, some of them deserters and criminals. It was never actually proved whether they were plotting rebellion against the Mexican authorities, but they were a potential powder keg. By April of 1840 Alvarado, the Mexican governor, had had enough of the swaggering insolence of Graham and his gang. He suddenly ordered his prefect, José Castro, to arrest and deport every foreigner in California who had either entered the country illegally or not married a native daughter. Unfortunately a few innocent had to suffer with the guilty. Among them were my great-great-grandfather, Arabella, and the baby Carlton. They had just two hours' warning, which they spent burying their few small valuables in an iron box in the ground. Before the night was over, the little family, with only Arabella's painting case and the baby's cradle, were huddled in a creaking cart on their way to Santa Barbara. From Santa Barbara the exiles were taken in a ship, the *Joven Guipuzcoana*, to San Blas in Mexico and thrown into prison at Tepic."

"Wasn't that against international law?" put in Doña Ysabel.

"It certainly was. But if it hadn't been for Eustace Barron, the British consul at Tepic, all forty-seven of the prisoners might have died of neglect and disease. But some of them were British, so Barron had a legal excuse to intervene. Through his efforts, the prisoners were finally released and acquitted, and even given small reparations."

"Did they come back to California?" asked Melinda, leaning forward eagerly.

"Would to God they had!" Robin's voice was leaden. "But the baby was ill, and Arabella frightened and homesick. So they sailed for England instead. Their ship was wrecked off the Scilly Isles."

"Oh, no," gasped Melinda. "Were—were they all lost?"

"There was only one survivor from the whole ship. A baby boy was found by a fisherman wedged in a wooden cradle among the rocks. How he had escaped is a miracle. He had golden hair which curled into a dark brown ringlet on top of his head, and a tiny mole on his right ear. Around his neck on a cord was a small jade monkey holding a coral pomegranate. Otherwise there was no name, no identification. But the moment that Arabella's father heard of the shipwreck and its one survivor, he journeyed to the Scilly Isles and took the child home with him. He had a painting of Arabella as a baby and there was the same golden hair with the dark curl. Also the boy was the right age. Anyway, he always believed that the child was his grandson. Before they left the Isles, the fisherman gave them a box which had been washed ashore after the wreck; it was Arabella's painting kit with her name inside the lid. In it were her paints and sheets of ivory ... and one finished painting."

"Painting of what?" asked Melinda.

Robin smiled. "Three generations have sought the answer to that question. And it's why I'm in California. According to family tradition, it's a sort of coded guide to where the iron box was buried. Arabella must have painted it on the long voyage home to England so that she wouldn't forget the exact location, but she coded it so that any unscrupulous fellow passengers who might be returning to California ahead of her wouldn't know the secret."

"Apart from family interest," put in Doña Ysabel, "are those few small treasures so important?"

"Yes, señora. Because Arabella's father never adopted the shipwrecked baby legally, and he died without a will. At his death, a cousin turned up from Australia and claimed the estate. Carlton contested him; he wrote dozens of letters trying to unearth evidence that Arabella *was* his mother, but Mexico and California had gone through great upheavals in those thirty years. The ship's passenger list had been lost; there was no one who could swear that Arabella's baby had a mole on his right ear, or wore a jade monkey on a cord around his neck. Carlton lost his suit."

"Was he married?" Melinda wanted to know.

"Yes, very happily. And as he became successful in business, he got over his disappointment at losing the estate. He bought a beautiful Queen Anne house called Courts of the Morning, became lord mayor of a big city in the North of England, and was knighted. However, fortunes don't last forever, and Carlton's son was a much-loved clergyman who succeeded in giving most of it away. My father, the clergyman's son, just managed to keep Courts of the Morning and the land around it by becoming a gentleman farmer and working himself to the bone. But then"—Robin's voice was carefully expressionless—"he was killed in the war. Now, between death duties and rising costs—well, it's a familiar story in England today. But I don't intend to let the place go without a fight." He lifted his chin stubbornly. "Mother isn't well, her sight and hearing are failing. It would kill her to have to sell Courts of the Morning and start over. And . . . and it's my *home*," he finished. "It's worth any gamble."

"So," summed up Doña Ysabel, "you've come to California, hoping to dig up the buried chest and with it the evidence to prove that your great-grandfather was Arabella's son, and then fight for his estate which went to the Australian cousin?"

"Well, not exactly f-f-fight." To Melinda's amazement, a flush was spreading under Robin's tan. "I mean, I know I s-s-stand a really good chance if I can turn up some proof. But I've been everywhere," he hurried on, "and I'm no further ahead. I was even having a good look around Sonoma that day when I found it was way past lunchtime and had to ring you!"

Melinda gave him a tiny smile. "I knew you weren't buying razor blades, since you use an electric razor."

"Miss Sherlock Holmes!" murmured Robin, but Doña Ysabel interrupted, "Is the estate enough to save Courts of the Morning, Robin? Perhaps it has dwindled like yours."

Robin grinned suddenly. "An old sea captain, señora, once settled a debt he owed Arabella's father with a deed to a slice of the Canadian wilderness. Nobody's ever been able to sell it, thank heaven. A few years ago they discovered uranium on it."

"Uranium!" breathed Melinda. Then her mind leaped back to the events of the past few weeks. "Robin, could anybody want to *prevent* your finding the iron chest?"

Robin stared at her. "I—I never thought of that." His voice trailed off. "It does seem as though somebody might be after . . . . No, it's too ridiculous."

However, Melinda noticed that he was very grave for several minutes as though there were something disturbing in the idea.

"Do you have the painting with you?" asked Doña Ysabel.

"I have a color photograph of it. The original is in Coutts' Bank in the Strand in London." He drew a fountain pen from his inside pocket, unscrewed it, and took out a closely rolled tube of paper which he handed to Doña Ysabel.

Over her godmother's shoulder Melinda studied the fantastic picture, painted with a miniaturist's precision.

To the left was a design of water with a gold disc in it, while more water slanted downward toward the right in a finger shape. Standing on a point of land between were three extraordinary figures dressed in brocades and crowns, with a pile of—Melinda bent closer—surely those weren't *oyster shells* at their feet? At the top left were ten barrels stacked above a curly blue line that ended astonishingly in an American flag. A little distance away was another ribbon of water, this time inhabited by several fish swimming wearily upstream. Below the fish were two little cottages, prim and plain and as alike as a salt-and-pepper set.

And that was all, except that in the upper center, between the American flag, the barrels, the fish, and the cottages, were three trees and a rock. The trees were painted as vividly as a botanical exercise; Arabella was making sure that no one mistook that tall California redwood, the fluttery willow beside it and, forming the point of a rough triangle, the smooth red bark and tiny blossoms of a manzanita tree. At the foot of the triangle stood a large rock and perched jauntily atop it was an old-fashioned flatiron.

"*Bueno*," announced Doña Ysabel briskly. "Let us start with the obvious"—she tapped the left of the picture—"that must be the Pacific Ocean because the sun is setting in it. The wide finger of water is an estuary. The gentlemen in gold crowns must be the Three Wise Men."

"*Three Wise Men?*" repeated Melinda.

But Doña Ysabel did not stop to explain. "The fish are swimming upstream, so that means they're salmon." She pointed to the two little cottages. "What do you make of those?"

"Nothing," replied Melinda and Robin in unison. "Except," added Melinda, "that they look like one house which has been sliced down the middle and served up in two helpings."

"Not surprising," remarked Doña Ysabel, "because that's what they are." At their bewilderment, she laughed. "On a rancho east of Rancho Bodega James Dawson and Edward McIntosh built a house in—in 1834, I believe it was. About five years later McIntosh received a generous land grant and Dawson did not. In a fit of the sulks Dawson sawed the house in half and had his section towed by oxteam to a new location. Melinda, bring me your map of Northern California."

Melinda was back with it in a few seconds. As Doña Ysabel unrolled it to Marin and Sonoma counties, Melinda cried suddenly, "There's the finger of water—Tomales Bay!"

"Which is famous for its oysters. And there"—Doña Ysabel tapped Point Reyes Station—"are the Three Wise Men. Originally it was Rancho Punta de los Reyes, named for a point of land meaning Point of the Kings, or the Three Wise Men." The jeweled finger traveled up the map. "Estero Americano, the American Estuary—hence the flag. And there is Salmon Creek. Here is where Dawson divided the house. And that pile of barrels in Arabella's painting"—she pointed to Bodega Bay— "*Bodega* means a cellar or wine vault. So—somewhere in the not-too-large area between Bodega, Salmon Creek, and the American Estuary you must search for a redwood, a willow, and a manzanita with a great rock at their feet. Beneath that rock, if the Holy Angels smile on you, you will find your buried box of iron."

Robin looked as though it were all a dream and he was afraid to wake up. He gazed down at the little old lady, fragile as a valentine in satin and lace, and whispered, "*Gracias, bella señora*, with all my heart."

At the same moment the clock ponderously struck one, like a night watchman yawning. Doña Ysabel rose to her feet as though it were a summons. "Come, Robin, you and I will go around the corner to the car and tell Miguel, if we can waken the lazy rascal, that I am ready to leave."

"*Leave*, Doña Ysabel?" gasped Melinda. "But you can't drive back to Colina de Oro tonight."

The old lady smiled. "I can and I will. No one but you and Robin will ever know that I was here. The fewer spoons in the pot, the less stir." She kissed Melinda. "Tell no untruths, of course, my child. But I do not expect that your parents will *ask* if Doña Ysabel was here this evening." Leaning on Robin's arm, she went to the door. "If I were you, I should not wait too long to go exploring. *Buenas noches*, my children."

"Good night," whispered Melinda. "And . . . and thank you, dearest."

Her heart on wings of joy, Melinda flew back to the living room. She smoothed the sofa pillows and put the map away. Then, just as she heard the whoosh of the family's Buick pulling up in the driveway, she ran upstairs to her room.

A moment later the side door clicked and Robin came bounding up the back stairs. "She got off safely," he whispered. "We'd better get some s-s-sleep. We'll need an early start." His face was glowing and his stutter betrayed his excitement. "Oh, Melinda, I can hardly believe it!" Before she knew what was happening, she found herself swung off the floor in a jubilant hug.

Then Robin disappeared down the hall to his own room, leaving Melinda with her heart swinging on a star.

CHAPTER FIFTEEN

The Search

THE house was still asleep when Robin and Melinda tip-toed down to the kitchen next morning. Robin was wearing khakis, boots, and an ancient tweed jacket which had originally come from Savile Row, but it had come a long, long way.

Petunia greeted them in surprise. "Ah thought you-all wouldn't be down until noon."

"I don't suppose they-all will be. But we-all are hungry."

There was a lilt in Melinda's voice that made Petunia glance up. *Those chillun are up to some devilment,* she thought.

She was sure of it the next minute when Melinda said coaxingly, "Petty, could you"—Melinda never called her "Petty" unless she wanted something—"could you fix a picnic for us, pretty please? It's such a gorgeous day that Robin and I thought we'd drive into the country."

"Humph, mah little toe says it's fixin' to rain." Petunia's broad forehead wrinkled in thought. "But Ah got some fried chicken left over and some potato salad, and there's a couple of apple turnovers . . . ."

"Sounds all right to me." Robin grinned. Then he stopped at a curious muffled thump in the hall.

They turned to see the Baron de Palafox limping into the

kitchen on his crutches. He beamed at them. *"Bonjour! Bonjour!* You are surprised, yes? We arrive home so late last evening that your generous parents insist I stay ze night."

"I'm glad," said Melinda impulsively. She was fond of the funny little Frenchman.

Petunia called from the stove, "You get the baron's coffee and roll, chile. Ah'm busy with your picnic."

"Peek-neek? What peek-neek?" asked the baron with sudden interest.

"Oh, it was such a lovely day that Robin and I thought we'd drive into the country."

"Ah ha! How *romantique!*"

To her annoyance, Melinda felt herself blushing. After a quick breakfast, she hurried upstairs to slip a note under her mother's door, saying that they were going on a picnic and not to worry if they were late getting home. Then she fished a coat from her closet, dropped purse, scarf, and flashlight into the pocket, and ran downstairs again.

Robin was waiting at the car with the picnic basket.

When they were on Lombard Street heading for the Golden Gate, he remarked casually, "I hope you know the way, Melinda, I don't."

Melinda gulped. "Honest, Robin, I'm an awfully dim navigator. Daddy says he'd rather be lost than have me giving him directions—it's less likely to give him a stroke." She unfolded the map. "I—I think we cross the bridge first."

"That's good news," replied Robin with a poker face, "because Lightnin' Bug isn't much of a swimmer. Then what?"

"We go through San Anselmo and Fairfax to Olema . . . I guess."

"A bit more conviction in the voice, please, Miss Marshall."

"I . . . I'll try!" Then she gave a little stretch of excitement. "Oh, Robin, wouldn't it be wonderful if we did find—what we're looking for?"

Robin didn't answer, but his hand reached over and closed around hers.

After crossing the bridge and leaving the Waldo Tunnel behind them, they saw the crest of Mount Tamalpais rising above foothills brown with the summer sun. Then just before San Rafael they turned off the main highway and drove through the small green-and-white towns of Ross, San Anselmo, and Fairfax. After Fairfax the towns became countryside, sometimes thickly wooded, sometimes open grazing fields, and the road grew narrower. After the whoosh-whoosh of cars speeding past them on Highway 101, traffic thinned out. Even the air smelled different, the scent of hay and eucalyptus was spiced with the tang of the sea.

At Olema they turned right on Highway One. Melinda felt her heart skip a beat at the sign *Point Reyes Station, Tomales, Bodega.* She knew that never again would she see those names without thinking of a tiny bright painting and Doña Ysabel's voice unraveling the fantastic puzzle.

At Point Reyes Station they took the right fork of the road, leading along the east shore of long, finger-shaped Tomales Bay. They passed a cluster of summer cabins, melancholy and deserted in the September sunshine. A peeling sign said OYSTERS. Here and there along the inlet maple trees were striking their autumn matches against the green hillside.

Robin glanced at his watch. "By Jove, it's quarter to twelve. I'm hungry."

Slowing down into a turnoff overlooking the Bay, he switched off the engine. The green taffeta sea was torn into white flounces on the rocks below them; to their right one lone and twisted cypress leaned landward, less a tree than the shape of the wind made visible.

Robin drew a deep breath. "How glorious! It reminds me of Cornwall. The water and those purple pincushiony thistles and the color of the sky are just like Tintagel. That's where King Arthur lived, you know."

"That's where King Arthur is *supposed* to have lived." Melinda was always a stickler for accuracy.

Robin replied loftily in his Englishman-laying-down-the-law-to-a-mere-female voice, "That's where he *did* live. And someday, when I take you to Cornwall, I shall prove it to you."

Dearly as Melinda relished an argument, this subject seemed to be leading onto dangerous ground. She shied away with "There's a bay not far from here where another famous Englishman spent a whole winter once with his ship, the *Golden Hind*."

"Sir Francis Drake?" asked Robin in surprise. "What was he doing here?"

"Well, when he sailed from England in 1577 with five small ships, he *said* he was going to trade with the East. Everybody knew that was just Drakese for plundering Spanish ships on the high seas. But the *Golden Hind* got separated from the others in a storm and sailed up the Pacific Coast, exploring. Drake missed San Francisco Bay in the fog; he went on, to a little inlet below Point Reyes which is still called Drake's Bay, took possession of the land for Queen Elizabeth, and named it Nova Albion. His chaplain went ashore and said the first Episcopalian service on the North American continent there as well."

She stopped to unscrew the jar of potato salad. "Robin,

what are we going to do when we get to Bodega? How shall we start?"

Robin finished a chicken leg, then threw the bone far out into the Bay with an effortless curve that would have told an English girl at once that the thrower was a first-class cricket bowler. "We must stop at a farm and ask if they know of a redwood, a willow, and a manzanita growing close together with a big rock at their feet, or even just a redwood and a rock, for the manzanita and the willow may not have survived after all this time."

"What reason do we give?"

"We're botany students from the university," replied Robin promptly, "and there's something unique about that particular redwood. They don't know how unique," he added with a boyish grin.

"What if the farmer doesn't know of it?"

"We'll just keep on asking until somebody *does* know."

After tossing their crumbs to the sea gulls, they were on their way again.

Only once as they rolled down the ribbon of road toward Bodega did Melinda think of the man in the mask and the warning in Chinatown. But if there were the slightest danger, she knew that Robin would not have let her come with him. As he said, why should anyone try to prevent his finding the iron box? Out here, with no other cars on the road for miles, and the clean tang of the autumn air, and the wide, windswept curve of coast below them, it seemed more unbelievable than ever. So she lifted her face to the sun's warmth and erased the bad dream.

But it wasn't quite so warm as it had been before lunch. The fringe of clouds had grown until they were no longer small and white and fluffy, but gray and cold along the horizon. An urgent wind had sprung up.

"Looks as though it might rain," remarked Robin. "Petunia's little toe was right."

They stopped at the first farmhouse in Bodega. But the farmer had never heard of a redwood with a big rock at its foot.

They went a few miles farther and asked again. And again. And again.

As the afternoon wore on, past two o'clock, past three, it seemed to Melinda that they must have covered every inch of the countryside, while the clouds piled up in great menacing banks the color of steel wool. She tied on her scarf tightly and tried to hide her growing discouragement.

At last, after they had asked more than a dozen times, they found themselves on a narrow track that ended at a cliff overlooking the ocean. An old man was trudging along it. His eyes were faded from squinting through wind and weather; the years had written deeply on his tanned skin. At his heels trotted a golden Labrador whose expression said that he knew his master was crazy to go for a walk in this weather, but that was all the more reason why he needed a faithful companion.

On impulse, Melinda exclaimed, "Robin, let's ask *him*."

The old man was the first person they'd spoken to who looked neither suspicious nor amused. "Lucky you asked me. I'm probably the only man in Sonoma County who could tell you where those trees used to stand." He smiled reminiscently. "They were all together, in a triangle like, with this big rock between 'em. They were in a dip where the water runs heavy after a big rain, and one year the willow got washed away." He scratched his head. "Can't remember what year it was nor what happened to the manzanita. Spindly little no-'count tree. But the redwood now, ah, she was a beauty. Tall and straight and old as America."

"Is it still th-th-there, sir?"

The old man shook his head. "Struck by lightnin' she was. Around twenty year ago."

"You mean there's nothing left of any of them?" Melinda's voice was almost a wail.

"Reckon the shell's still standing. And the rock."

"Where exactly is this g-g-gully from here?" asked Robin, only his stammer betraying his excitement.

The old man squinted down the road. "About two mile of this here lane, then there's a right turn. That road takes you across the main road and just after it there's a cattle gate on your left."

Melinda got out paper and pencil.

"About twenty yard after the gate you'll see a track leading into a field. It says KEEP OUT, but pay no mind, the bull died couple o' year ago. Follow that track until you come to land that's never been cleared. Through it on the right you'll see an old trail"—he looked down at Lightnin' Bug—"reckon you can make it," he added unflatteringly. "At the end you'll come to the gully. Better not drive down into it, too steep. The shell of the redwood'll be on your right and the big rock is just below it. You can't miss it. And . . . ."

But the rest of his sentence was drowned in a far rumble of thunder. He smiled at them. "Must be on my way. There's a real storm coming up and I like to be out at the headland for it. Captained a windjammer once . . . never miss a storm if I can help it. Good luck to you."

"Thank you, sir," replied Robin with a fervor that only Melinda appreciated. The old man was already hurrying on toward the cliff, the Labrador close at his heels.

They drove on carefully, too excited to talk, except for Melinda's brief directions. Another growl of thunder shook the air. Robin glanced at his watch. It was nearly four o'clock.

They saw no one as they took the right turn, crossed the main road, passed the cattle gate, then turned into the track through the field and entered the grove of trees, which appeared to be a small forest, dark as twilight under the pewter sky. Branches brushed the canvas top of the car that Robin had put up when they stopped. The woods became darker; they almost missed the trail branching off to the right, the trail which the old man had said led to the gully.

It was barely more than a path, furrowed by rains in the spring, bordered by sky-screening trees. The little car struggled on bravely but the noise of its puffing and grinding was louder than the gusts of wind. Robin bent tensely over the wheel.

They were both so intent on the road that they never once looked back.

If they had, they would have seen another car inching through the trees behind them and a pair of dark eyes watching as they turned down the lonely trail to the gully.

CHAPTER SIXTEEN

Watcher in the Rain

BUMPING along the twisty trail, Lightnin' Bug finally reached the edge of the gully.

"Bother, it's dark as the jungle," exclaimed Robin as he switched off the engine.

Getting out of the car, Melinda shone her flashlight along the tunnel of trees and underbrush. Only an occasional spurt of wind plucked the interlaced branches here; otherwise it was quiet. *Too quiet*, thought Melinda. It had the prickling stillness of a locked room. A scurry among the leaves made her jump. But it was only a family of California quail scuttling to shelter before the storm, their black-feather topknots bobbing anxiously like question marks over their heads.

"Where shall we st . . . ." began Robin.

But before he could finish, a sudden dazzle of lightning ripped across the sky. For one second every twig, every crumpled leaf was etched with a glittering needle of blue light. The thunder followed almost instantly, tumbling around them like an avalanche of rocks. At the first crash Melinda found Robin's arm around her shoulders. She clung to him unashamedly.

Then, as the roar muttered away to the horizon, she heard

his excited: "Melinda, did you see it? The *redwood!*" Grabbing her hand, he pulled her after him into the gully.

There the flashlight outlined a gaunt half shell of bark, its inner surface still black from the flame that had once devoured its heart in just such a storm as this. Twenty feet downstream rose a great rock shaped like a crouching cat.

"Oh, Robin, it is! It *must* be!" Melinda's breath caught with excitement. "Hurry! Where's the shovel?"

"Confound it! I left it in the car!"

While she waited for him, Melinda began moving the smaller stones away from the base of the boulder until another jab of lightning sent her ducking close under the overhanging rock.

Then, little by little, faster and faster, the rain began. Heavy drops pushed the dry leaves apart with a sound like crumpling paper. Soon the dusty gully was a mire of mud. Melinda pulled up her collar, but it was as though a faucet had been turned on above her. She had never seen such a cloudburst.

The pelting rain made so much noise on the leaves and pebbles that Melinda didn't hear the faint snap of a twig as stealthy footsteps slipped behind the redwood from the far side of the gully.

She only saw Robin returning from the car with shovel, pickax, and trowel.

She chose the pickax and went around to the other side of the rock. "You dig in front and I'll dig here and we'll have twice the chance of finding it in half the time. At least"—she frowned—"I *think* that's what I mean."

Squinting through the rain which was now a driving torrent, she set to work. After a little Robin's voice came to her around the rock. "Found anything?"

"Water," replied Melinda grimly. "What have you struck —oil?"

His answer was lost in a growl of thunder.

Fifteen minutes later they had dug their way entirely around the rock down to hard shingle. Discouraged, they stopped for breath and a consultation.

"What do we do next?" asked Melinda.

Robin wiped the rain out of his eyes. "Start building an ark?" There was now actually a stream at the bottom of the gully, rushing over the small stones, swirling in an eddy where it met the rock. "This must be a real river in the spring when .... What's the matter?"

Melinda had suddenly grabbed his arm. "Robin, *that's it!* In some flood the rock has been washed downstream. In Arabella's painting it was right at the foot of the redwood, not here. We've been digging twenty feet from the spot." Her eyes were shining.

He caught her eagerness. "Come on. We'll try again."

They scrambled upstream. Rain, blisters, weariness forgotten, they set to digging with new energy at the foot of the blackened shell. Robin wedged Melinda's flashlight into a V of bark in the redwood stump. But they'd hardly started to dig when it sputtered out.

"Blast!" exclaimed Robin. "Sorry, Melinda. Why didn't you tell me that your torch wasn't waterproof?"

"I didn't know," she replied sweetly. "Up to now I've always gone swimming in daylight."

Laughing together, they went on digging. Five minutes ... ten ....

And then suddenly Melinda's pickax said *poing* instead of *ske-woosh.*

For a minute she didn't know what had happened. Then, when she realized that she had actually hit *metal*, she cried out "Robin!" and began scrabbling frantically.

The way she said it made Robin jump to her side.

At the next clink of metal on metal, Robin flung away his shovel. Heedless of the mud, he fell to his knees and set to work with the trowel.

It was too dark now to see anything more than a hole of blackness.

"There are matches in my hip pocket," directed Robin. "See if they're dry enough to light."

Melinda struck one, then sheltered it with her hand against the rain. It lasted only a second.

But it was enough to show them a glimpse of a box at the bottom of the hole.

Rusty, muddy, but unmistakably a box.

Melinda's heart was thumping. Neither of them spoke. Neither of them glanced up.

So neither of them saw the shadow watching close behind them, motionless as a spider.

"A root's holding it," muttered Robin. "When I say one, two, three, I'll pull the root away and you get a grip on the box. One, two"—he leaned on the coil of root—"three!"

The next second Melinda was standing erect with the iron box in her hands. "*Robin!*" she breathed. She couldn't believe it.

"Good show." Robin was scrambling to his feet. "Now the next...."

His sentence was sliced off by a last dagger of lightning down the sky.

And Melinda looked up to see a man in a long black rain-coat looming in front of her.

A man without a face. Two slits in a white mask flickered hungrily over the iron chest she held in her hands.

Her scream was swallowed up in the crash of thunder.

CHAPTER SEVENTEEN

Pursuit

IN the slash of lightning Robin saw Melinda's terrified face. He sprang to his feet as the darkness fell again like a shutter.

Clutching wildly at the iron chest, Melinda jerked backward.

But she was a second too late. A pair of hands had lunged for the box.

Frightened as she was, she still noticed that one of those hands had a long, recent cut across the deeply calloused palm.

Then she screamed again.

With one leap Robin was at her side. There was the crunch of a fist as Robin sent the man in the mask staggering backward.

But the man recovered with the quickness of a cat and grabbed once more at the box.

This time Melinda's foot slipped in the mud.

The stranger snatched the chest as she fell, spun on his heel, and was across the gully in two leaps.

With a yell Robin flung after him. The thief had a head start, but Robin was the faster.

Melinda dashed after them. She was twenty feet away when they came to a small clearing among the trees.

Here Robin, a bare yard behind the thief now, thought he saw his chance.

He tensed, measuring the distance. Then, with a huge burst of speed, he vaulted forward in a flying tackle.

But as he sprang his heel caught in a root. Crashing to the ground, his outstretched hand missed the other's ankle by inches.

The thief glanced back.

And in that instant Melinda first saw someone else standing in the path ahead of them.

Someone else . . . .

She caught her breath, telling herself it was a trick of the slanting rain and the shadows.

But it wasn't. A new figure had emerged from the floor of the forest as though he were . . . waiting for them.

The fugitive caught sight of him too late to dodge. A powerful twist and the iron box went spinning out of his hands. The thief found himself sprawled in the mud, his arms pinned behind him.

Robin tried to struggle to his feet, only to fall back.

Melinda ran to him. "Robin, what is it?"

"My ankle." He gritted his teeth. "Never mind that. Have you got the box?"

Before she could answer, there was a shout ahead. Throwing off his assailant with the strength of panic, the man in the mask had leaped to his feet and escaped toward the main road.

The iron box still lay where it had fallen in the mud.

For a moment his pursuer seemed about to race after him. But, instead, he turned back to where Melinda was bending over Robin.

Clenching his teeth in fury and pain, Robin dragged himself to a sitting position. "Quick, man, he'll get away!"

It was too dark to see the man's face, but both Robin and Melinda were aware of a slight shrug of his shoulders. "Not far, I think," he replied pleasantly. "And if I did go after him, ... did you think you could escape with that ankle?"

Escape? Melinda lifted her head. Something about that chilling half-voice, half-whisper was familiar. "Who ... who are you?"

"My name is Herbert Lee," said the stranger formally. "You are Miss Melinda Marshall, your English friend is Mr. Robin Sutherland, and you have both caused me a great deal of trouble." Drawing a powerful flashlight from his pocket, he shone it down at Robin. "I fear that Mr. Sutherland has sprained his ankle." He stooped to examine it, his face in shadow behind the light. "I shall bring my car as close as possible. Miss Marshall, will you help me to lift him into it? I know you would not be so foolish as to try to ... move ... before I return." He then picked up the iron box. "I shall take care of this. Later, when you are more comfortable, we will open it ... together."

A shiver passed through Melinda. The moment he was gone she leaned down. She could not see Robin's face, but his hand was gripping hers fiercely. "Does it hurt very much?"

Robin's reply was prompt, *and so British*, she thought with a throb at her heart. "Not terribly. But I could think of pleasanter places to be lying. Although some people actually take mud baths on purpose, I've heard." He lowered his voice. "Melinda, who *is* he? And where is he taking us?"

She could only shake her head in the darkness and cling to his hand.

In less than two minutes they heard the approaching purr of a car. It pulled up close to them, rain shining in front of the headlights like cellophane fringe.

Mr. Herbert Lee left the driver's seat and came to them. "Put your arm around my shoulder." He leaned down. "Miss Marshall will be on your other side. There. Now take it slowly." As he spoke, he lifted Robin to his feet with surprising strength and lightness.

Melinda and Robin obeyed him. There was nothing else they could do. Slowly the three of them covered the few feet to the open door of the car.

The headlights stabbed Melinda's eyes. She turned her head away. As she did so, she looked across Robin to the man on the other side. For one instant Mr. Herbert Lee was clearly outlined in the car's lights.

And Melinda's ankles turned to straw.

He was Chinese, with a downward droop in his left eyelid.

CHAPTER EIGHTEEN

A Box of Shadows

HELPING Robin into the car, Melinda felt dazed, trapped. Half of her mind wanted her to run for her life. The other half numbly obeyed the silken voice of Mr. Herbert Lee; and she found herself sitting on the front seat with the precious box lying between her and the Chinese.

She did manage to ask as he started the engine: "Where are you taking us?"

Herbert Lee paused. Then: "To Colina de Oro, I think," was his astonishing reply.

Colina de Oro? Surely she hadn't heard correctly. Why would he take them there? In her incredulous joy and relief, Melinda forgot that, except for a shifty-eyed foreman and an old, old lady, Colina de Oro was as remote, locked away in its valley, as any secret hideaway.

The car edged forward past Lightnin' Bug, forlorn under the dripping trees. Close to the main road Herbert Lee pulled up. A man had emerged from the dimness.

"Got him?" asked the Chinese.

Melinda saw the nod. "Doesn't fit your description, though." The man peered into the car. "That the girl?"

Melinda shrank down.

Lee's only answer was, "The party was bigger than I expected. We are going to Colina de Oro. Bring the yellow MG there."

As they emerged from the forest, Melinda saw with astonishment the pale, melon-gold twilight which still hung over the open countryside. "What time is it?" she asked.

"Only half-past six." The Chinese smiled. "When one is idle, time plays the tortoise. But when one is busy, time is a dragonfly. You and Mr. Sutherland have been very busy this afternoon."

Minute by minute the miles flew past them. Suddenly Robin spoke from the back seat. "Mr. Lee," he asked in a voice taut with pain, "are we your . . . prisoners?"

The Chinese took his eyes from the road to glance reproachfully at Robin. "*Prisoners?* What an unpleasant word, Mr. Sutherland!"

But that was all he said.

Melinda murmured, "Did your . . . friend . . . catch the man in the mask? The one who escaped?"

"Of course."

"Do . . . do you know who he is?"

"No. Do you?"

She shook her head.

Ten minutes later the car crested the rise looking down onto Colina de Oro. For the first time Melinda thought of the effect their surprise visit might have on Doña Ysabel. She put in quickly, "Mr. Lee, my godmother is nearing ninety. I . . . ."

He turned the car down the incline. "She shall not be alarmed, I promise you." Then a hint of amusement crept into his voice. "But you underestimate the Doña Ysabel, I believe. It is doubtful whether Joaquín Murrieta, the great

California outlaw himself, could have alarmed her. She would have told him to put away that silly gun and wipe his boots properly."

And he was right. As soon as the car pulled up in the half-circle of wet gravel before the rancho, the great River of Life door with its massive hinges swung slowly open. Silhouetted in the square of light from the hall stood Doña Ysabel.

"Is that you, my child?" she called across the drive.

To Melinda, worn out with strain and fear, there was nothing surprising about the question. Of course Doña Ysabel knew. She always knew.

Before anyone could stop her, Melinda had jumped from the car, run across the drive, and flung both arms around her godmother's neck.

"Did you find the box?" whispered Doña Ysabel.

Melinda nodded. "But somebody tried to get it away from us, and then . . ."

"Your assistance, please, Miss Marshall," called Mr. Lee sharply. The words were polite but the tone was a command.

Melinda returned to the car. Together she and Mr. Lee helped Robin across the gravel. The Chinese had the iron box under one arm.

If Doña Ysabel was startled at the sight of the man whom she had last encountered outside her bedroom window now assisting Robin into the house and unmistakably taking charge, she gave no sign. She merely led the way to Robin's old room and drew back the spread on the bed.

"Sorry to be such a nuisance," apologized Robin, "but I did something stupid to my ankle."

Doña Ysabel laid cool fingers on his forehead. "Lie down, my son. Melinda, two hot-water bottles. You, sir . . . ."

"This is Mr. Lee, Doña Ysabel," put in Melinda.

Mr. Lee bowed, as though there were nothing incongruous about formal introductions at this moment, and shook hands. Whereupon he had the surprise of his life. The pale and slender hand extended to his was about as fragile as tempered steel. Doña Ysabel gave him her sudden sparkling smile, murmured, "You are in your own home, señor," and then went on briskly giving orders. "You will find clean pajamas and a dressing gown in that closet. Melinda and I shall return in a few minutes. Come, child."

In her own room Melinda slipped into dry clothes and found a minute to telephone home. It was a worried Petunia who answered. Mr. and Mrs. Marshall had gone down the Peninsula after luncheon. Her crossness over the phone betrayed her relief.

Melinda just told her that Robin had sprained his ankle and they would be spending the night at the ranch. For the rest of the story she wanted to tell her parents first.

When she and Doña Ysabel returned to Robin's room with the hot-water bottles, a cup of herb tea and bandages, they found Robin changed to pajamas, propped up in bed. Herbert Lee was looking at the iron box on the table.

After Doña Ysabel had applied her special ointment to his ankle, which filled the room with the pungent prickling smell of eucalyptus and camphor, bound it with linen strips, and plumped up Robin's pillows, she sat down by the window, serene as a nun in her long black gown, and said, "Well, where do we begin?"

"With the most important thing?" suggested Herbert Lee. He lifted the box from the table. Setting it in the middle of the floor, he knelt before it, brought out his pocketknife, and set to work with oriental patience.

Robin watched him from the bed, his hands clenched in frustration. This was the supreme moment of his search, the climax of a lifetime's work and planning, and he had to lie powerless on a bed and watch a heavy-lidded stranger open *his* box, *his* dream.

Melinda saw the suffering tighten his mouth. She let her hand rest on his shoulder in wordless sympathy, and his fingers came up to close gratefully over hers.

The box was about eighteen inches long and ten deep, with a close-fitting lid. Herbert Lee worked his knife blade under the hasp and bent his strength to it. A click, a rusty screech, and the lid grated wide.

Melinda was the only one watching the Chinese instead of the box. She saw his face go blank with amazement.

A Spanish shawl was folded over the contents of the chest. Carefully he lifted this out, examining every fold. Underneath were several small packets, a long shape folded in a sheet of yellowed paper, and a book. One at a time he removed them and, in silence, laid them in a row on the table, minutely searching each article before he put it down.

A pair of rose diamond earrings, a gold bracelet, a black baby cup which had once been silver, a locket of twisted hair, a prayer book, a fan with carved mother-of-pearl guards . . . .

And that was all.

Melinda felt Robin's hand loosen on her fingers, then fall heavily to his side. She looked down at him. The light had gone out of his eyes and for one unguarded moment heartbreak was bleak in every line of his face. There was no clue here to the identity of Arabella's baby son. A journey half across the world, for a pair of earrings and a faded fan. Melinda wanted to put her head down on his shoulder and cry.

Herbert Lee was still examining each item with a swift, practiced skill. When he looked up at Robin there was a new expression in his enigmatic eyes. "I should be grateful, sir, if you would tell me your story of this box."

But before Robin could answer, Doña Ysabel had leaned forward. "I think we deserve an explanation from you first, Mr. Lee. Who are you and what are you doing here?"

A smile played over the face of the Chinese as he reached into his pocket. Drawing out his identification, he handed it to the older woman.

"I am a T-man, señora," he said dryly, "a Treasury narcotics agent."

CHAPTER NINETEEN

Anonymous Tip

N ARCOTICS agent?" gasped Melinda. "But you've been
following *us!*"

"Orders." Herbert Lee nodded briefly. "Apparently I wasn't
the only one. There was quite a procession today." He smiled
suddenly, a boyish, rueful smile that changed his whole expression. *Why, he's almost as young as Robin,* thought
Melinda.

"Orders? What orders?" demanded Robin.

"To find out what you were *really* doing in this country."

"Did you have orders to whisper frightening warnings to
me, too?" put in Melinda indignantly. "And to interview
Miguel at three o'clock in the morning?"

The Chinese-American looked embarrassed. "When else
could I talk to him—in private? However"—he spread his long
hands in a gesture of defeat—"in spite of my reminding him
of his unsavory police record which he has kept hidden all
these years, he makes up in one virtue what he lacks in others,
and that's loyalty. He refused to say one word about any of
you. As for the warning, I certainly did give it to you, Miss
Marshall. You had just had a narrow escape from a runaway
truck which may or may not have been an accident. I risked

passing on to you a Chinese proverb, which you have disregarded completely," he added dryly.

"Warning?" Robin sounded stunned. "Against whom?"

"You, sir."

"*Me?*" Robin sat up in the bed, winced, and lay back.

"We had been informed that you were—dangerous," remarked the agent. "However, it might be helpful if you told me your story first."

Robin began unwillingly. But little by little, under the searching eyes of the T-man, he found himself telling Herbert Lee the full story of his inheritance and search and the two encounters with the man in the white mask.

When he had finished, Herbert Lee smiled. "It's such an incredible story, it must be true. And yet it doesn't answer the one important question: why should the Bureau of Narcotics be asked to watch you, and by whom?"

Robin's eyes were as blank with bewilderment as they had been the night before when Doña Ysabel asked him who could want to prevent his finding the iron chest. "I haven't the slightest idea."

"When you entered California," Herbert Lee went on grimly, "we received an anonymous tip that you were not just a young British writer, but the agent of an international dope ring. We were told that you would travel all over California establishing contacts with other agents, that eventually you would lead us to the source. The tip was apparently a smoke screen for someone else's activities: a most foolhardy and dangerous thing to do. However, California has a big narcotics problem—we can't afford to ignore a single tip. But after a short observation I became more suspicious of the tip than of you. *Until this afternoon!* When you began digging for something in the middle of a cloudburst, my confidence took a nose dive. And when you actually dug up an iron box ... !"

"I have a question," put in Doña Ysabel. "I can understand why you might be trailing Robin. But what were you doing outside of my bedroom window?"

"A quiet round of inspection, Doña Ysabel. The Bureau doesn't miss any angle." Mr. Lee suddenly chuckled. "I've had some surprises in my career but none of them, señora, can match your gracious, 'My friend, what is it that you seek?' spoken in the dark hours of the morning out of what I had thought was empty shadow!"

Before Doña Ysabel could answer, the telephone on the bedside table jangled. Herbert Lee reached swiftly across for it.

"Hello. Yes, this is Lee." A pause. Then his face tightened. "*What?*" There was an icy edge to his voice that made Melinda glad she was not the man at the other end. "That is no excuse. Send out an all-points bulletin at once. I'll be there in half an hour. Tell the sheriff to send a man to Colina de Oro for the night." He hung up. "The fools," he exploded, "the stupid, blundering ...."

Doña Ysabel gave him a small wise smile. "So the man in the mask escaped?"

"He did." Herbert Lee bit off the words. "They paused for a stop light and apparently he just dived out the window."

"Don't scold them too hard, Lee." Robin's smile was rueful. "He's as slippery as a peeled tomato. I've had an encounter with him, too. He specializes in the surprise getaway."

"Well, he won't get very far," the Chinese announced grimly. "They had stripped off his mask before putting him into the car, so they have a description. And he was bare-handed, so they'll get fingerprints."

"His right hand is cut across the palm," remembered Melinda suddenly. "It's very calloused, but the cut is recent."

"Good, I'll add that. It's just a matter of hours, I'm sure. Meanwhile, I must get back to headquarters as soon as the sheriff's man arrives."

He said it casually, but Melinda leaned forward. "You mean you think he'll make for Colina de Oro?" she asked in a whisper.

Herbert Lee gave her what was so obviously meant to be a reassuring smile that she felt suddenly shivery inside. "Oh, no, but until he's recaptured I'm not taking any chances. After all, he knows you've got the box and whatever's in it."

"Whatever's in it," echoed Robin with a bitter laugh, looking down at the iron chest lying open on the floor. "Nothing."

Melinda sat up. "Are we *sure* it's nothing? Maybe the man in the mask knows more about it than we do. I'm going through it myself."

She knelt on the floor and as the others watched she started in with the shawl. Then she borrowed Doña Ysabel's magnifying glass and looked at the earrings. She went over every stick of the little fan. She turned the pages of the book.

But she had no more success than Herbert Lee.

Despondently, she slumped back on her heels.

And then Doña Ysabel said quietly, "Have you measured the chest itself?"

There was a tingle of significance in her husky murmur that sent Melinda diving forward again. After one glance she cried excitedly, "The bottom inside, it's not down enough." She laughed shakily; her words always played leapfrog at crucial moments.

Swiftly Herbert Lee handed her his pocketknife. She worked it down between the bottom of the chest and the silk wall, and pried.

It was stiff. She moved the knife, tried again. There was not a sound in the room. But across the valley an owl cried Whooooh! Whooooh! out of the stillness.

Melinda tried once more.

And the bottom suddenly came loose in her hands. It was a false panel and underneath was an inch-deep compartment.

In it were two small packets: a tiny box and a flat black case.

Melinda was scarcely aware that she had opened them. She only knew that the boxes were suddenly lying in her lap. Laughing and crying at the same time, she was lifting up their contents for Robin to see; and there was something in her throat so that she couldn't say a word.

In the box was a tiny jade monkey holding a coral pomegranate between its paws. The flat black case opened to reveal a miniature of a little boy—a boy with golden hair and a queer dark curl on top, and a small mole on his right ear.

CHAPTER TWENTY

Good-by, Robin

NO one spoke for a full minute.

Then Melinda whispered to her godmother, "Doña Ysabel, how did you guess about the secret compartment?"

"Because my mother had an iron box just like this one."

Herbert Lee picked up the jade monkey. "This is Chinese. Arabella's husband must have gotten it from an oriental trader. They were probably a pair of pendants for a ceremonial sash."

Robin was studying the painting with a mixture of affection and wonder. "Arabella *was* a good artist. This could be a miniature of the portrait her father had painted of the little boy he brought home from the Scilly Isles wreck."

"Do you really think there's enough...." Melinda hesitated.

"Proof?" finished Robin. "I don't know. But I'm going to fly home as soon as I can and find out!"

Melinda's heart sank. And yet, what else could she expect? Robin's search was over. There was nothing to keep him in California.

There was a swish of wheels in the driveway. Herbert Lee went out while Melinda replaced each item in the iron box.

When the Chinese-American agent returned, he had two

men with him, the deputy sheriff who would spend the night at Colina de Oro and a policeman.

"I must be getting back," he told them, "but I wanted Frank to read you the description of our fugitive and see if you could add anything."

Frank thumbed through a notebook: "Height about five feet ten. Weight around one-sixty. Age twenty-five to thirty-five. Eyes gray. Hair light. Complexion pale. Distinguishing marks: recent cut on palm of hand. Exceptionally agile. Last seen wearing dark raincoat."

Mr. Lee turned to Robin, Melinda, and Doña Ysabel. "In other words, a man who looks exactly like everybody . . . and nobody," he said with a grim smile, "average height, medium weight, youngish, face as blank as wax, who is undoubtedly no longer wearing a shiny black raincoat!"

The following morning Robin's ankle felt better. Herbert Lee telephoned that he had made a reservation with BOAC for the next night. There was no news of the man in the mask. Melinda managed an early-morning visit with Silver-stockings, but the deputy sheriff accompanied her to the stables. And when it was time to leave for San Francisco, a plain-clothes man drove them in Herbert Lee's own car. Lightnin' Bug would be brought down later and garaged at the Marshalls' until Robin could write to them what he would like to have done with it.

There was a world of warmth in Robin's voice as he said good-by to Doña Ysabel and thanked her "for . . . for *every-thing*." She reached up her thin white fingers to his face and kissed him on both cheeks. "God go with you, my son," she whispered huskily.

The ride back to San Francisco was gloriously sunny after the storm, with a freshly laundered blue sky. There were autumn wood smoke in the air and firecracker bursts of dahlias and chrysanthemums in the gardens they passed. To Melinda, sitting beside Robin and the precious iron chest, the ride had never passed so quickly. She could hardly believe that those scarlet cables against the sky were the Golden Gate Bridge already.

They had decided only to tell Mr. and Mrs. Marshall that they had gone on a picnic and got caught in a cloudburst during which Robin had sprained his ankle. The car bringing them home and later taking Robin to the airport was to belong to "a friend of Robin's"; and Mr. Lee had agreed that the Marshall house was to be policed unobtrusively. If anyone noticed . . . well, there had been several burglaries on Pacific Heights lately and the police were being extra vigilant. There was no point in worrying Mums.

It was Petunia who opened the door to them. "Ah sho am glad to see you-all!" Her smile of welcome pleated a dozen tucks up her cheeks. "Mrs. Marshall and Miss Honey Rose, they'se havin' luncheon on the porch."

Leaving Petunia and the plain-clothes man to help Robin and his luggage to the guestroom, Melinda raced up to the third floor and burst out onto the porch.

If Mrs. Marshall were startled at the fervor of her daughter's hug, she gave no sign but only remarked tranquilly, "Have you had lunch, Baby?"

Honey Rose wasted no time on non-essentials. "Where's Robin, darling?"

The same old Honey Rose! "He's downstairs. Yes, thank you, Mums, we've had lunch."

"How long will he be here?" Honey Rose had a one-track mind.

"Until tomorrow evening." At Honey Rose's sudden glow, Melinda couldn't resist adding, "When he flies back to England."

"To *England?*" wailed the Southern girl.

Melinda buttered a muffin. "You sound as though he were taking a rocket to the moon. England's not so far away," she remarked airily.

Honey Rose said nothing, but she nibbled thoughtfully at a stalk of celery, and her expression announced that a good deal of ground was going to have to be covered in the next thirty hours.

Just how much ground Melinda did not realize until the following evening.

She had noticed in the course of the two days that Honey Rose contrived never to be farther than ten feet away from Robin during all his waking hours. There was nothing obvious about it—Honey Rose was too skilled for that—she was just always *there*, lovely, languid, and wearing a different dress for each meal.

Using his ankle as an excuse, Robin didn't leave the house, or the iron box, during the two days. A policeman quietly patrolled the block. Herbert Lee telephoned twice a day to report, in a more and more baffled voice, that the man in the white mask had vanished into thin air.

Robin did not invite anyone to the airport to see him off, but told the Marshalls that he hoped they would come to England before too long. "There's a direct flight from San Francisco to London now, you know."

"Think of it," said Mr. Marshall, "and in 1860 all the West

was agog over the Pony Express, Sacramento to St. Joseph, Missouri, two thousand miles, in nine days! And now it's less than a day to London."

"I wonder if any of us are any happier?" sighed Mrs. Marshall.

"*I* certainly am," replied Robin. "Wasn't it five dollars for half an ounce on the Pony Express? Let's see, I weigh twelve stone—sorry, I mean one hundred and sixty-eight pounds! That would be around a hundred and twenty-seven thousand dollars. Whew!"

The car was coming at seven. At six o'clock Robin went down the hall to Melinda's room. Under his arm he had the iron box. "Would you look after this for me, please, Melinda? I'm taking the miniature and the monkey with me. The rest I'll leave here in the chest. The trinkets aren't valuable, but I know Mother would like to have them someday, and I can't take it now."

Melinda reached out her hands almost reverently. He was giving his dearest treasure into her keeping. "I'll watch over it for you as long as you want me to, Robin," she whispered.

"Thanks awfully, dear." He paused and seemed about to say something else. But, instead, he only laid his hand on her shoulder for a minute before limping back to his own room.

Half an hour later, his luggage ready by the front door, Robin's voice drifted from the kitchen, giving Petunia Romeo's farewell: "*A thousand times good night!*"

Then Melinda heard him exclaim, "Bother! I must have left it in my room," and his uneven footsteps ascended the stairs.

The minutes dragged past. Mr. and Mrs. Marshall were in

the living room. Melinda kept glancing at the clock. "How awful last minutes are!" she was thinking to herself when the doorbell rang.

"We're a minute early," Herbert Lee greeted her.

"Robin's ready. He'll be right down." Then, as her parents came out to the hall, she introduced Lee as "a friend of Robin." In a city where many of the young executives are Chinese or Japanese and most San Franciscans have oriental friends, it never occurred to them to be surprised.

Mr. Lee carried Robin's luggage down to the car. Mrs. Marshall turned to her daughter. "I wonder what's keeping Robin?"

"Maybe he didn't hear the doorbell. I'll run see." Melinda hurried up the stairs. But Robin wasn't in his room. He wasn't in the hall. She looked everywhere. Then she thought of the outdoor porch. Perhaps he had gone out for one last glimpse of his favorite view.

She ran on up to the third floor. The door at the end of the hall was ajar. "Robin, the car's h . . . ."

She turned the corner, and stopped.

Robin was indeed out on the porch. With Honey Rose.

Just as Melinda saw them the Southern girl turned to him and murmured something in her caramel drawl. Robin looked at her for a long, serious moment.

Then he leaned down and kissed her.

Melinda felt as though she had been struck.

Without a word she turned and stumbled blindly down the stairs. It couldn't be true. It couldn't . . . .

But it was. And it was like a knife in her heart.

CHAPTER TWENTY-ONE

Debut for Melinda

ROBIN'S departure was a heartbroken blur for Melinda. When he took her hand warmly, lingeringly, she felt the tears stinging behind her lids. *I won't cry,* she thought fiercely, *I won't cry.*

But after he was gone and she could fling herself on the bed in her own room, tears would not come. Crying was for little-girl hurts. This was too deep, too bitter. Memories crowded into her mind: Robin lifting her hand to his cheek in the car, Robin carrying her after she fell from Silverstockings, Robin. . . .

But it was Honey Rose whom he had kissed good-by.

She buried her throbbing forehead in the pillow. Was it her fault that she had believed Robin felt more toward her than—than a brotherly affection?

And yet he had shared his dearest secret with her, she had helped him to find the iron chest. Of course a tomboy *would* be better at a day's hard digging than a Georgian beauty. She had been what Robin needed, he had taken her help, he had given wings to her heart . . . and now he was gone, with a farewell kiss for Honey Rose.

She did not sleep that night. But by the time the early sunlight filtered through her curtains she had made up her mind.

She must forget him.

She wouldn't tease or question Honey Rose. She would never mention his name again. It meant tearing out the brightest pages of this summer, but she had to do it. Robin would become only a bittersweet memory, a part of growing up.

At breakfast the next morning Mrs. Marshall was startled at Melinda's breathless: "Mums, could we have Jimmy Carter to dinner, please?"

"Why, of course, dear, if you'd like." Mrs. Marshall shot her daughter a keen glance, but Melinda was spooning brown sugar onto oatmeal with her eyes lowered. "I'll ask if he can come over for supper tonight."

The invitation to Sunday supper was accepted by Jimmy Carter with enthusiasm. He greeted Melinda, and Petunia's pancakes, appreciatively, and he had the surprising tact not to mention Robin Sutherland. The following day he was being promoted to vice-president of his father's company, so he did not stay late, as his father had dropped a ten-ton hint that it might be a good idea if the new vice-president were at his desk on time for the first week at least. But when he left, he enclosed Melinda's hand gently and awkwardly in his great St. Bernard's paw. "Don't forget, Lindy, I'm still around."

Melinda was touched. "Thank you, Jimmy. You're very sweet," she whispered impulsively.

Jimmy vented his feelings by draping his arm around her shoulders and nearly crushing the breath out of her.

It was not the last evening Jimmy came to supper that autumn. And although she still felt numb inside, Melinda began to count on Jimmy as an escort to the parties that gathered speed up to the debut season at Christmastime.

Another person who took to dropping in for a few minutes "on his way home" was Herbert Lee. Ostensibly his visits were to tell her the news, but as there never was any—the man in the white mask had done an uncannily thorough job of vanishing—she soon decided that he called because he liked it.

Then one evening, when Melinda was alone in the house, he arrived with news. "We've got something to go on at last. We know his name."

Melinda did not need to ask whose name.

"Scotland Yard had his fingerprints. He's an Englishman named Hugh David Phelps. The name mean anything to you?"

Melinda shook her head. "I've never heard it before."

"Well, Scotland Yard has. And they would like to question him about some unsolved cat burglaries a few years ago. I'm going to cable Robin. We'll track down Hugh David Phelps if it takes ten years."

But when he telephoned later with Robin's reply, she was not surprised. Robin had never heard the name either. "Sorry," he had wired back, "but my circle of acquaintance seems painfully limited. I don't know many cat burglars."

Melinda herself had had several letters from Robin, but she found it too hard to answer them, and they finally ceased. She wondered if Honey Rose heard from him, but she wouldn't ask. And nobody commented that she didn't skim down the stairs at the postman's morning ring any more.

The task of erasing Robin Sutherland from her slate was even harder than she expected. She might shut the gate to her heart and hang a No TRESPASSING sign on it, but everything she touched, every place she went, she heard Robin's voice in her ear or saw his slow, lopsided smile. When she received her long-hoped-for acceptance from Stanford, it wasn't quite the same when she couldn't share it with him. Even long rides on Silverstockings through the Lagunitas hills did not bring a happy heart...she was always thinking of their twilight ride together.

To keep busy, she flung herself into all the preparations for her debut. And that event which up to now had been an awesome date in the misty future was suddenly just weeks away and then—like a snowball rolling down a hill—only *days*.

San Francisco's debut season is at Christmastime, centered around the Debutante Cotillion. The girls who make their curtsies at the Cotillion are chosen by a committee, not for wealth or social showiness, but because they come from respected old California families. Melinda's own personal debut was to be an old-fashioned tea a week before Christmas.

On the morning of "D-day, D for Debut," as Mr. Marshall called it, the first florist's box arrived before Melinda was even up. She knew it was traditional for the friends of a deb to send bouquets for her big day, but tradition is something you read about. This was *real*.

She tore off the cover. Inside were two gorgeous white orchids with hearts the color of Sutter's gold. The card said: *For Lindy on her great day. Hope these get there firstest with the mostest. Love, Jimmy.*

She laughed. The flowers did look like Jimmy, just a little larger than life.

After breakfast Mr. Marshall left for Colina de Oro to bring Doña Ysabel to San Francisco for what everybody kept calling her first trip away from the ranch in fifty years. Melinda smiled to herself and kept her secret.

Next the decorators arrived. Soon an eight-foot Christmas

tree rose in the curve of the staircase, gaily polka-dotted with nosegays of red carnations. In the drawing room garnet roses lighted every corner, and near the piano stood the traditional "orchid tree" to which were tied the orchids sent to Melinda for her big day.

After the florists left, Melinda stood wide-eyed in the middle of the room and drew a deep breath. Was it real, or was it a shimmering dream from which she'd wake up any minute? This fairyland of flowers, the beautiful tree, that special dress waiting upstairs, all of them to celebrate her grand entrance upon the stage of grownupness.

"Exciting, isn't it?" remarked a familiar voice behind her.

She whirled. "Doña Ysabel!" Flying across the room, she enveloped the black-satin figure in a hug. "I'm so glad you're here!"

Doña Ysabel began, "For you, dear, I would..." but she was interrupted by the doorbell again.

It was another florist's delivery boy, only this time the box was small and precious looking.

Inside, crisp as starched lace against the pale green tissue, Melinda found a nosegay of lilies of the valley. She drew out the card.

> *Muquet de bonheur, lilies of happiness. In my country, the flower of a beautiful young girl. From your old friend, Henri de Palafox.*

"How lovely. And so like him to send something different." She buried her nose in their sweetness.

"Melinda," a voice called over the banisters, "it's half-past three."

"Coming, Mums."

Melinda knew better than to offer Doña Ysabel her arm as they went upstairs together. She had done it just once and been told to keep things like that for old ladies.

Dressing, even for such an exciting event, did not take Melinda long. Twenty minutes after she stepped out of her shower she was all ready in embroidered organdy the color of hyacinths, short white gloves, and the heirloom enamel cross on its chain around her neck. As she got out the dyed-to-match slippers from the back of her closet, she touched the iron chest. She turned away quickly, closing her heart to the rush of memories. There was no time for those today. . . .

Then she hurried down the stairs and out to the pantry where her bouquet waited in the refrigerator. It was an old-fashioned nosegay of bouvardia and garnet roses with a silver ruffle.

Returning, she met her mother coming down the stairs. Mums paused on the bottom step for a full minute, gazing at Melinda as though she were a stranger. Her eyes suddenly misty, she held out her arms. "My grown-up baby!"

They clung tightly to each other for a moment.

And then the bell rang.

Mrs. Marshall dabbed at her eyes as she and Melinda took their places in the drawing room. Majestic in starched apron and her "Sunday gray" dress, Petunia sailed in to open the door to the first guests, and the party had begun.

It seemed barely ten minutes before the room was filled with people. Doña Ysabel joined the receiving line in black velvet with a great collar of creamy lace that fell over her shoulders. Honey Rose helped shepherd the guests out to the dining room whence came delectable smells of hot lobster puffs, fruitcake, ginger, jasmine tea, candied violets.

After a while Melinda began to feel that she was in a play, endlessly rehearsing the same line: "Thank you so much. I'm so happy to see you. Thank you for your lovely flowers. Thank you . . ."

She looked up to see Jimmy Carter in the line, and winced. For ordinary conversations his handshake was enough to unscrew the bolts on a flat tire, but for a special day like this . . . . "Hello, Jimmy." She smiled apprehensively.

She was right. Jimmy took her little white glove in both hands and held it, as she afterward said, "as if he'd fallen over a cliff and I was the rope."

"Gosh, Lindy, you look great!"

But Melinda prized that statement more than any of the flowery compliments she'd received. It was so painfully, perspiringly sincere.

Shortly after, Melinda glimpsed Herbert Lee in the line. Beyond him was the Baron de Palafox. Although his progress on the crutches was as labored as ever, the Frenchman's mustache and goatee gleamed with pomade, and in honor of the occasion he was sporting a new brocade waistcoat. Two or three people stepped out of line, making him go ahead of them.

Melinda heard his low voice murmuring, *"Merci, merci bien."*

With a bow, Herbert Lee also stepped aside and motioned the crippled man ahead of him.

"No, no, you must not," protested the baron.

"Mais oui, monsieur, j'insiste . . . ."

Melinda listened in surprise. Did Herbert Lee speak French as expertly as he did everything else?

And then the person in front of her had passed on, and the Baron de Palafox, his crutch caught under his elbow, was holding out his hand to her. "My dear Melinda . . . ."

She started to take his hand. Then, for some reason, she glanced down at it first.

And the room whirled around her. She stared at it, unable to move, unable to cry out. *It couldn't be*. Herbert Lee was watching her with sudden trigger keenness.

The hand of the Baron de Palafox was deeply calloused from gripping the handle of the crutch. And across it was a long, recent red scar.

It was the hand of the man in the white mask.

CHAPTER TWENTY-TWO

Disguise

"H AS it occurred to you," remarked Doña Ysabel after the last guest had left, "that the initials of Hugh David Phelps were the same as those of Henri de Palafox? I suppose he was taking no risk with old monograms."

The Marshall family, Honey Rose, Herbert Lee, and Doña Ysabel were gathered in the the drawing room. Melinda, pale from shock and sickness of heart, was lying on the sofa. It couldn't be the baron! The family friend who had sent her lilies of the valley—charming, gallant, funny old Henri de Palafox.

But it was. The baron had been escorted from the room by Herbert Lee so quietly that none of the guests were even aware of it. Then, later, the narcotics agent had returned to fill in the details. The baron, fingerprinted, stripped of his disguise, had confessed. Briefly Herbert Lee sketched in Robin's story for the rest of the family.

"*But why did Henri do it?*" demanded Mr. Marshall.

Herbert Lee leaned back in his chair. "Hugh David Phelps is a man cursed by laziness, an actor's skill, and the moral backbone of an earthworm. The combination has led him to explore every avenue of riches without work. However, cat burglary in England proved so unlucky that he had to flee the country one jump ahead of Scotland Yard. He came to San Francisco, adopted an elaborate disguise, mustache, goatee, gray hair, and called himself a baron. Without make-up he's an ordinary, nondescript little man, the ideal type for impersonations. He chose this city for his new career because he had heard—forgive me—that San Franciscans are dazzled by titles and fall over each other to entertain them."

Mrs. Marshall smiled embarrassedly. "I'm afraid that's often true."

"He thought a French baron ought to be good for an unlimited supply of dinners and weekends. Part of the act was to read up on California and pose as an authority. With this, plus wit and flattery, his meal ticket would be assured. And then a trinket here and there might disappear, enough to pay his rent. The limp was a touch of genius—a cat burglar is the most athletic of all criminals. Who would dream that an ordinary blond, clean-shaven young thief, if he were ever spotted, could possibly be the same as a cripple with gray hair and a goatee? A quick change into the baron, and he would be safe. But as it turned out, he didn't have to steal any trinkets, after all, or so he swears. He started giving lectures and charging a fat fee for them, and after a while he settled down into what he called respectability. Whether cadging dinners from gullible society hostesses could be called respectable is open to question, but at least it does not come under police surveillance."

"We have such a big French colony here in San Francisco," said Mrs. Marshall, "how could he have deceived *them?*"

"He had spent part of his boyhood in Paris. And he had an actor's ear for an accent. However, did you ever notice that sometimes he spoke much better English than at others?"

Melinda broke in for the first time. "But how did he get mixed up in—in *this?*"

"You must remember that he was really an Englishman. He subscribed to a London paper. One day he read about Captain Robin Sutherland, a young Guards officer, who had become a national hero in the recent war against the terrorists in Malaya."

Melinda sat up. Robin—a *hero?* He'd never even mentioned . . . .

Honey Rose, too, was leaning forward, her eyes glowing.

Herbert Lee saw their surprise. "Didn't he tell you? Robin holds Britain's highest military decoration. But you can't live on decorations. After he left the Army, some of his friends petitioned Parliament to restore Carlton's estate to Robin as a reward for valor. After the Australian holders of the estate died out, it had passed to the nation by what lawyers call *escheat.* The request was favorably received, but Parliament asked for some proof that the little boy found by a Scilly Isles fisherman was actually Arabella's son."

Suddenly Melinda knew why Robin had been so reticent when telling Doña Ysabel that he wouldn't exactly have to f-f-fight for the estate.

"You know the remainder of Robin's story," went on Herbert Lee. "He was too modest to tell you that the estate was to be returned to him for his heroism. But when the English papers carried the story that proof was needed and then mentioned that Robin was coming out to California for a visit, Hugh David Phelps put two and two together and guessed that proof was to be found here. Always at the back of his head has been a dream of returning to England with a fortune in a character which no one, least of all Scotland Yard,

would ever connect with Phelps the cat burglar. Dinners and
lecture fees in San Francisco were not enough to achieve *that*.
And here was a young man with a fortune dumped in his lap
—if he could prove his inheritance. What simpler than imper-
sonating this young man with his own uncanny skill at imita-
tion and make-up, returning to England with the proof, and
claiming the estate? Needless to say, there were tremendous
risks, but Phelps was a gambler, and these were high stakes.
However, his dramatic flair carried him too far; he promptly
made his fatal mistake of informing us, anonymously, that
Robin was a courier in an international dope ring. His idea was
to discredit Robin, but he must now deeply regret ever having
invited federal authorities into the story."

"What"—Melinda's lips were dry—"was he going to do *if
his plan succeeded?*"

"Return to England, prove the inheritance, collect the
money part of the estate as quickly as possible, then make himself scarce and begin life somewhere else in a new disguise. If
Robin turned up, Phelps would accuse *him* of being the im-
postor. No, it's not as fantastic as it sounds. Remember Phelps'
plan hinged on his finding the proof *first*. After that, it would
be only Robin's word against his. Phelps could do a lot of
boning up on Robin's background. Robin has no living rela-
tive except his mother whose sight and hearing are failing.
War always changes a man, and very few of Robin's particular company came out of Malaya alive. Phelps gambled on
no one being positively able to swear that he was not Robin.
There were several cases in the war, you know, of skilled
agents being able to deceive even a man's wife and children."

It was Honey Rose who put into words what they were all

thinking and dared not say aloud, "Wouldn't he have tried to kill Robin first?"

Herbert Lee looked at her. "At heart," he replied soberly, "Phelps is a coward."

Melinda nodded. "Yes, because in the storm we were powerless. He could have"—she shuddered and closed her eyes—"but he ran away."

The Chinese-American agent went on quickly: "He found out from the British consulate where Robin was staying. Then, in his own character, without the make-up and crutches, he tracked him, recognizing him from pictures in the English paper, always watching for an opportunity to steal whatever map or plans Robin must have with him. After that I think you know the rest of the story."

"But the truck?" murmured Melinda. "Was that Phelps' work?"

Herbert Lee spread his hands in a futile gesture. "He says not. But it would have been so easy. He could have had a good search for the plans on Robin if he'd been hurt, under pretense of giving first aid. *You* would never have recognized him. On the other hand, it was the most incredible luck for him to meet Robin at your party that evening. He could study him at his leisure, pick up his characteristics. Then he learned that Robin had a car, and he thought the plans or map might be in the car or the luggage. That was why, the following day, he siphoned the gas out of Lightnin' Bug and replaced just enough to get Robin out into the country. The idea was that when Robin hiked off to a gas station, he'd search the car. Only two things went wrong. Robin took you with him, and the MG went much farther on the small amount of gas than he had calculated. He was going up to Santa Rosa for a lecture, as the baron, of course, so he wore the mask for safety. Later, in the storm, he wore it to frighten you. At breakfast that morning you had talked of a picnic, so he just followed you."

"But after he escaped from your men," put in Melinda, "he never seemed to try anything more."

Lee smiled. "It was all getting a little hotter than he liked. I told you he was a coward. The risks were getting too great."

Mrs. Marshall pressed her hand to her forehead. "Poor Henri," she whispered. "Poor, silly, gallant Henri. It's all so . . . tragic."

"Crime is always tragic, Mrs. Marshall," replied Herbert Lee gravely. "However, if you saw Hugh David Phelps as himself and not dressed up as the baron, I don't think you would feel he deserves your pity. It is not a gallant elderly cripple we are arresting, but a youngish man sufficiently nimble to have made a career of second-story burglary. Forget the character of the attractive French nobleman; he never existed. And now"—Herbert Lee stood up—"I must go and cable Robin Sutherland the news. I think . . . I think he might be interested," he finished in a classic understatement which matched some of Robin's own.

CHAPTER TWENTY-THREE

The Curtsy

THE excitement of parties, Christmas shopping, and the Cotillion rehearsal (Jimmy Carter stepped on her foot only twice, a record for him) whirled Melinda through the following week. *My heart may be empty*, she thought wryly, *but my calendar certainly isn't.*

Christmas itself was the one quiet day. All the family, including Petunia, opened their gifts in front of the fireplace in the living room. The fire was burning with its own festive reds and blues and greens from the sea-salted driftwood which the Marshalls always gathered on the beach especially for Christmas Day. After dinner Mr. Marshall read aloud the Christmas story from the Gospel according to Saint Luke, and then they sang carols around the piano. Melinda listened to Petunia's deep, heart-tugging voice singing "Oh Come, All Ye Faithful," and something of the star-shining wonder and joy of this greatest birthday of all stole over her. For the first time since Robin had left, she found peace in a forgotten corner of her heart.

Early on the morning of the second day after Christmas twenty-six girls in twenty-six San Francisco homes slipped out of bed and hurried to the window. And twenty-six an-guished voices chorused: "Oh, *no!*"

It couldn't rain today, the day of the Cotillion. It just *couldn't!*

By lunchtime the fates that plan the weather had been re-minded by twenty-six fervent prayers that this was not just an ordinary day, so they turned off the wind and rain and turned on a sparkling winter sun.

Petunia was the only one who had not been dismayed. "My little toe wasn't fussin', I knew the rain would stop."

Melinda spent the morning practicing her curtsy to the grandfather clock in the hall, and going down the stairs until she could do it without glancing at her feet.

She had to be at the French Parlours of the Sheraton-Palace Hotel at seven o'clock in the evening, so at three she started dressing.

She had just finished her shower when Honey Rose came in. "Will you tell me, pet, what you think you're doing?"

"I'm getting dressed. I have to be there at seven, and it's past three now."

"And you'll barely have time to throw on your things and dash!" Her cousin grinned. "Have you thought what you're going to do between half-past three, when you'll be ready down to the last eyelash, and quarter to seven, when you leave for the Palace? Go for a long walk in the living room? You won't want to muss your skirt by sitting down."

Melinda plopped onto the bed beside her. "All right, you win! I'll wait until . . . until five o'clock."

"You make it sound about forty years away. Believe me it'll come soon enough!" Honey Rose stood up from the bed with the lazy grace that was part of her Southern blood. "Good luck, darling."

Five o'clock actually did arrive at last, and it was time to slip into the creation of moonlight, stardust, spun sugar, and angels' wings.

When she was all dressed, it was a new and radiant Melinda Marshall who made one last curtsy to her mirror. If only Robin could have seen her like this. Hurriedly, she pushed the thought out of her mind. But just before she went downstairs she turned back to her jewel case and slipped on the bracelet with the little gold lion he had given her.

At the foot of the staircase she had to give a "fashion show" for her family, who behaved as all families do at moments like these. Mr. Marshall harrumphed loudly that he was glad she liked the dress, because at that price she'd have to wear it for the next twenty years. Doña Ysabel instructed firmly, "Stand up straight, child, and *think proud*. Remember your ancestors came with Anza!" And Mums exclaimed "*Baby!*" and began to cry.

Despite Melinda's certainty that the car wouldn't start or they'd have a flat tire, Mr. Marshall delivered her safely to the Sheraton-Palace by five minutes to seven. The others would follow later for the dinner party Mums was giving, like so many other parents, in the Gold Ballroom before the presentations began at ten-thirty.

As the doorman opened the door, Melinda had a moment of panic. "Oh, Daddy, I ... I can't...."

Mr. Marshall's eyebrows shot up. "Can't what? You're a fine one to get an attack of nerves. What about *me?* Having to sit through a whole evening in a homicidal starched collar which will strangle me before you've even curtsied, and then skating across the dance floor to cut in on that heavyweight champion escort of yours. And you think you've got problems. Good-by."

He started the engine again, but just before she got out, he gave her cheek a pat. "Good luck, dear!"

Melinda smiled bravely and hurried into the hotel, conscious of admiring glances down the foyer. A vacuum-cleaner convention was meeting in the hotel, and several of the young delegates stopped still in their tracks and stared after the tiny figure in shining brocade, wondering if they were dreaming.

As Melinda reached the elevator, a familiar voice over her shoulder said, "Hi, princess, looking for a knight in shining white tie?"

"Oh, Jimmy, I'm so glad to see you," she greeted him breathlessly.

He looked her over and then delivered himself of his greatest compliment as though he had never thought of it before. "Gosh, Lindy, you look great. And ... and awfully grown up."

She smiled happily and slipped her hand through his arm.

They found most of the other debs and their escorts already in the French Parlours, as well as the society editors of the San Francisco papers with their kite tails of fidgeting photographers.

There were gay greetings for Melinda and Jimmy, and they were handed glasses of punch. Melinda was grateful for it; her throat had already begun to feel as though it were paved with sandpaper.

Another pair of debs arrived then, and that completed the twenty-six, to the obvious relief of the committee and the editors.

Melinda was glad when the photographs were over and the debs and their dates could go into their own private dinner. Five tables were set for them, with pastel cloths and centerpieces of a gilded manzanita branch hung with Christmas balls. There were giggles as each girl was given a snowy outsize napkin to tie around her neck. The committee was taking no chances on anyone getting a spot on her white dress.

The dinner was delicious, but it was wasted on Melinda. She was even slightly annoyed with Jimmy for so obviously enjoying every bite. Didn't men ever think of anything but *food?*

By the time the clock circled around to the zero hour of ten-thirty, Melinda had been keyed up for so long that she couldn't believe it had really come at last. A final combing of hair and pulling on of long white gloves, a reassuring farewell from their escorts, and the girls were handed their bouquets— identical old-fashioned nosegays of gardenias. Then they were shepherded into the elevator.

The elevator was quiet after the buzz of the French Parlours; nobody had small talk during these tense minutes. Next the girls were guided by the committee through the huge hotel kitchen to the spot where they would wait just outside the Garden Court. It did seem a little odd to be awaiting the great moment of one's life in a kitchen, but from the Court beyond Melinda caught the strains of background music. She drew a deep breath. Her fingers were cold around her bouquet.

In the Garden Court the lights blinked, signal that the presentations were about to begin. At the far end, seated on a special dais for the patrons and patronesses and the parents of the debs, Mrs. Marshall leaned forward. Her own heart was thumping like a hammer. Under cover of the lowered lights her husband reached across and gripped her hand. She smiled at him shakily.

All eyes were on the lacy, spotlighted arch at the end of the big ballroom. The escort of the first debutante moved to the foot of the little flight of steps leading up to it. The Cotillion director took his own place. The band slid into "A Pretty Girl Is Like a Melody."

There was an expectant hush.

And a small figure in creamy brocade and white violets walked slowly, gracefully, out through the golden bower into the glare of the spotlights.

In a clear, measured voice, the Cotillion director announced, "Miss—Melinda—Marshall!"

At the spatter of applause Melinda hesitated nervously. Then across the Garden Court came a ringing, full-throated cheer. It was from the dais at the other end, and it sounded suspiciously like Daddy. Her lips trembled in a smile.

And with that smile she forgot to be frightened. This was her moment, her never-to-be-forgotten moment. Doña Ysabel's *think proud* flashed through her mind. She straightened her shoulders and smiled into the dazzle of spotlights as she dipped a steady, perfect curtsy. The applause swept into a thrilling wave across the ballroom. It surged around her, lifting her heart in a rush of joy. This wasn't a cold, distant, critical audience. *This was her own San Francisco family.*

The Cotillion director stepped forward and handed her a tiny box, her Cotillion souvenir, a small gold charm for her bracelet engraved with the date. His eyes said "Well done."

She still had the steps to negotiate, but they no longer daunted her. Confidently, her head high, she moved down the three shallow steps to the little landing. Here her partner joined her to give her his arm for the remaining few steps.

Through the dazzling, powdery brilliance of the white lights she could not see his face. She only thought suddenly, bewildered, a little alarmed, *but that's not Jimmy. He's too tall, too thin.*

And then a warm, familiar arm was under her hand. And a pair of warm, familiar blue eyes were smiling into hers.

"Good evening, my d-d-dear Miss Marshall," whispered a husky voice close to her ear.

And proudly, smilingly, Robin Sutherland led the first debutante of the season out across the shining acres of the ballroom floor.

CHAPTER TWENTY-FOUR

Duet Under the Stars

STILL in a dream, Melinda took her place at the edge of the ballroom floor. Beside her the tall young Englishman was looking down with a tenderness in his blue eyes that set her heart racing. "R . . . Robin," she whispered.

"Dearest." His hand tightened on her arm.

They could say no more. Already they were conscious of curious glances from the audience. Questions flashed through Melinda's mind: Jimmy, Honey Rose, Mums. She did not search for the answers. This was all that mattered, this moment with her own Robin beside her for all her world to see.

When the presentations were over, ending with the tallest girl, the debs were given favors for the dance, and their escorts received silver wands. Then the band broke into the old-fashioned bars of the special Cotillion figures.

For the first time a doubt brushed Melinda's mind. Robin had not been here for the rehearsal. "Can you?" she whispered.

He smiled reassuringly. "Jimmy took me through the paces. Don't expect Fred Astaire, but I think I can manage."

And he did—marvelously, in Melinda's opinion. Of course her opinion was not exactly impartial. The figures ended with the men forming an arch with their wands and the girls emerging through the "tunnel."

After that, in the Cotillion tradition, the debs and their escorts danced the first regular dance together, alone on the floor.

Melinda fitted into the curve of Robin's arm, her amber eyes radiant. She didn't care who saw how happy she was. But at last, under cover of the music, she asked, "Why didn't you tell me you were coming?"

His hand pressed hers. "I couldn't. I wasn't sure whether I'd get here in time. And I didn't know whether you wanted to see me. You never answered my letters. I thought it might be better to take you by surprise. But my—business—was finished the day before yesterday."

"Successfully?" she whispered.

The response was one of his boyish lopsided grins. "Rather! It all worked out even more wonderfully than I had dreamed. Courts of the Morning is safe. And there's a bit left over. Enough for. . . ." He didn't finish the sentence, but his arm tightened around her.

She whirled across the floor on a cloud. "Oh, Robin, I'm so glad. And then you flew over?"

"I only arrived this afternoon. I saw in the paper who your escort was going to be, and I went straight to see him. I told him the situation."

The color in Melinda's cheeks deepened. She decided not to ask Robin exactly *what* he had told Jimmy.

"And he was a splendid sport about it. He said he'd grown up with you and he was awfully fond of you, but he'd known what was happening. He thought after I left that maybe . . . I gather he's seen quite a bit of you?"

Melinda nodded without answering.

"But when I arrived, well, he acted like an officer and a gentleman. He taught me the Cotillion steps in his flat this afternoon, and we arranged that I should be waiting for you after your curtsy. We thought it better than my turning up in the French Parlours where everything would need so much explaining."

"Did he clear it with the Cotillion Committee?"

"Er . . . he said to leave all that to him," was Robin's airy reply.

Melinda laid her cheek lightly on his shoulder for a minute. "Oh, Robin. I know I'm dreaming," she whispered.

And then, abruptly, she raised her head and looked him in the eyes. "*But Honey Rose?*" she demanded.

"What about Honey Rose?" asked Robin in surprise.

It was hard to find the words. "I . . . I thought you and Honey Rose . . . that was why I didn't . . . why I couldn't answer your letters." Her voice had become smaller and smaller under Robin's astonished stare.

"Where in the world did you get that idea?"

"You . . . you kissed her good-by." She couldn't bring herself to look at him.

"So that's it! I suppose Honey Rose told you?"

She shook her head. "No, I saw you. When I came up to tell you that the car had arrived."

His cheek brushed her hair. "My poor darling! If only you'd written me what was bothering you. It was all so simple. I had gone out for one last look at the Golden Gate and to make a little private promise to come back, when Honey Rose turned up. She said it had been nice knowing me, but she knew when she was beaten! And then she asked if I would do one little thing for her before we said good-by for keeps. Of course I said I would. After all, she was your cousin. I must admit I was pretty taken aback when she said, 'Kiss me, Robin ... just once.' But I was stuck, I had given my word. Then when I got downstairs, I could hardly kiss you good-by, with everybody standing around. But oh, Melinda, if you'd only asked me instead of...."

Melinda closed her eyes. "It's all right now, Robin."

She opened them to find someone cutting in. She was almost surprised to see that it was her father. He smiled quizzically at Robin. "Er ... seems to me we've met before somewhere?"

Robin grinned. "Hope you don't mind, sir?"

Mr. Marshall glanced at his daughter. "Not at all."

Robin lingeringly released Melinda and she danced around the room with her father. "Oh, Daddy, isn't it wonderful?" she breathed.

"Just so ... it isn't too soon," murmured her father into the golden wisp above her ear. "Give your mother and me a while to get used to the fact that our little girl has grown up."

According to tradition, after the fathers have cut in on their daughters, anyone may cut in on the debs for a few minutes; and then the dancing is open to the other guests.

Which was how Melinda found herself being piloted doggedly around the dance floor by Jimmy Carter. He towered above her, his face brick red.

Melinda gave him a little light-as-a-petal pat on the cheek. "Thank you, Jimmy," she whispered, "with all my heart."

He couldn't find the right words, as usual. So also, as usual, he vented his feelings in nearly crushing her right hand to pulp. "Aw, that's okay, Lindy," he murmured awkwardly. "We're just a couple of kids who grew up together."

Melinda knew the effort it cost him to say that. She whispered, "I'm wearing your gloves, Jimmy. I'll always keep them to remind me of a dear and generous friend. And Jimmy" —she buried her nose in her gardenias and took a deep breath —"let's go on being friends, may we?"

His face lighted. "Sure. I'll come and visit you in your castle or whatever-it-is. Maybe I'll bring Honey Rose with me!"

It was Melinda's turn to blush. "Shshsh!" she begged, glancing around to see if Robin had overheard.

But Robin had gone over to the table at which Doña Ysabel was sitting. She was holding court in a beautiful dress of ivory satin encrusted with jeweled medallions of Spanish lace. Her garnets had been replaced by a Renaissance cross of diamonds at her throat, and a diamond crescent blazed in her hair. She was receiving almost as much attention and admiration as the debs. She extended her hand for Robin to kiss with a twinkling, "Welcome back, Prince Charming!"

Robin bent over her hand. "The Sleeping Beauty awakens, señora."

She laughed with pleasure and flicked open a gold-and-tortoise-shell fan. "But only until midnight, Robin. Then ... who knows, perhaps I shall become once more just a sleepy old lady!"

"*That*, señora," replied Robin firmly, "you could never be!"

Robin glanced beyond her and found Honey Rose watching him. He went around to greet her and Honey Rose laughed uncertainly. "I did not think we would ever meet again."

"I should be sorry if we did not," was Robin's courteous reply. But Honey Rose knew it for what it was, only the small change of politeness.

Soon Mr. and Mrs. Marshall returned from the dance floor, followed by Melinda and Jimmy.

After a minute Mr. Marshall cut through the greetings and explanations and held up his hand for silence.

"Going to make a speech, darling?" asked his wife.

"Yes, I have something to announce. A surprise. You all think that this is a special day because of Melinda. So it is. But there's another reason, too. Perhaps even more important." With a flourish he produced a small jewel box from his pocket and presented it—not to Melinda, but to her godmother. "She's kept it the deepest secret, but today is Doña Ysabel's birthday. *Her ninetieth.* Happy birthday, darling."

There were gasps and exclamations. Several nearby tables had overheard and spontaneously they clapped, too.

Doña Ysabel looked stunned. A dot of pink appeared in both her cheeks as she took the box. For the first time in her life Melinda noticed that her godmother's frail, lovely hands were trembling. "I . . . I am overcome," she managed to whisper.

"*Ninety,*" breathed Jimmy reverently. "Gosh!"

Something in his voice made Doña Ysabel look up quickly. Then, as she lifted the lovely jewel from its velvet, Melinda noticed the familiar twinkle return to her godmother's eyes. She drew a quick breath, squared her shoulders, and confronted them like a queen. "I, too, have a little surprise for you. Never did I believe that I would confess it, but now—" she glanced at the box in her hand—"this jewel is too . . . *magnifica* . . . for a mere ninetieth birthday. It makes me want to be truthful." She turned to Mr. Marshall with her sparkling smile. "Like many men who deal in millions, my dear man, you are not very good at arithmetic. This is not my ninetieth birthday. *It is my hundredth!*"

Melinda sat down suddenly on the nearest chair.

Hours later, in the crisp coolness of before dawn, the Cotillion was over. Melinda tucked her billowing skirt into the narrow seat beside Robin in Lightnin' Bug. The top was up and the car was a tiny world for two. As Robin started the engine, Melinda leaned her head against his shoulder. They didn't say anything. They didn't have to.

The roads were empty and dew-shining as Lightnin' Bug chugged out to Pacific Heights.

When they came to the crest of a street, they could see below them the jeweled sweep of San Francisco curving away to the dark and secret waters of the Bay. Alone on the hilltop, the December night presented this glimpse to them, wrapped in glittering stillness, ribboned with lights, like a breathtaking Christmas gift stretching from sky to sky. For this moment all the city's beauty, its romance, its proud, tumultuous past, belonged to them.

Robin stopped the car. Drawing Melinda gently to him, he kissed her for the first time. And it was not a brief, perfunctory kiss.

"How does that feel?" he asked the tip of her left ear when it was over.

She nestled into the curve of his arm. "Tickety-boo, darling," she whispered.

www.ingramcontent.com/pod-product-compliance
Lightning Source LLC
Chambersburg PA
CBHW020635180626
46816CB00003B/975